# CINNAMON ROLLS, ELEPHANTS, AND NOTES FROM THE DEAD

## SHORT STORIES AND ESSAYS

**James Reid McCartney**

Cover image: SelfPubBookcovers.com/ Daniela

To Communicate with James McCartney:
growthskills@hotmail.com

Books are available through all online bookstores.

Publishing assistance by BookCrafters, Parker, CO
www.bookcrafters.net

# Dedication

Cathy Ann

# CONTENTS

# The Prize

I am a writer! This entitlement of merit is a declaration that rests on the accomplishment of having written and published a book. Though I had, for several years, written articles for a church newsletter, I never consciously thought of myself as a writer until after my book was published. I want acknowledgment for my work; I want respect and prestige! The best way to help achieve this, I decided, is by entering and winning a book award contest.

Buoyed by pride in my first book, a new self-confidence also unveiled itself. So, when presented with the opportunity to enter a writing contest, I quickly proceeded with the required enrollment so as not to be detoured by procrastination. I must confess it was my new confidence that drove me to enter my book in the contest. Indeed, I would not have registered the book if I didn't think it had merit. I want other people to experience the originality and writing in the thought processes.

Fires of self-confidence had been stoked within me by several different people who, after reading my book, said they thought it was excellent. One of my friends, a poet, even remarked that he felt it was excellent poetic prose on par with some of the masters. However, by way of a modest disclaimer, I have tried not to listen to such praise. Why have I found it so difficult to close my ears to the flattery? Perhaps it was because I wanted to believe it.

The topic of my book compares a non-traditional religious philosophy, New Thought, with contemporary philosophy, Existentialism. When the two schools of thought are compared, within each is reflected personal authenticity and empowerment through self-responsibility. Choice and commitment establish the first movements of endeavor toward authenticity (self-actualization) and individual creativity. In consideration of these things, one can only wonder, how is it possible for such a book not to win?

As the awards banquet drew near, a little voice of doubt grew increasingly louder. I fervently wondered to myself, "What am I doing here?" From the very beginning of this adventure, I had made the decision that my book would best fit in a category called "Religion and Spirituality," but I began to question if it was well placed. It then seemed perfectly evident that I should have either chosen the "Philosophy" or the "Self-Help" category.

The event took place in a large open area of an art gallery. Twenty-two tables each seating six people. The majority of the participants were from the writing and publishing business. The literary organization's president, who organized the function, stood at the podium and described the process and rules of the contest. There would be three winners in each category, the winner of the first prize was to give an acceptance speech of thirty seconds or less after being photographed receiving a documented form of recognition from the president of the organization.

As a finalist assuming I'd won, I sat at my table listening to the above process while my mind was taking imaginative trips to the podium for acceptance of what I thought was a well-deserved reward in recognition of my book. The categories, presented in alphabetical order, gave me time to listen to the previous acceptance speeches. I began to formulate my own.

Each time a new winner would march to the podium and give their brief acknowledgment of thanks, I would change my mind, one way or another, about what I intended to say.

One lady spoke as if she was the recipient for the role of Leading-woman Actor at the Academy Award: "I want to thank (so on and so forth) and I want you to know that I am pleased to be recognized for all the hard work I have put forth. I want all you people in the audience (you little people, I thought to myself) to know that you too can achieve success as I have with hard work." It was probably not her intent, but it seemed to me that she thought she was the only writer in the room who mattered or had written a book. The truth is, the dear lady was happy and excited, and I was envious.

It seemed to take an eternity as I impatiently waited for the master of ceremonies to get through all the awards preceding my category, and when the time came, I felt I was ready. I said to myself, my book is excellent. I'm a finalist; they understood it. They know all the hard work that goes into producing a book. Keep your acceptance talk simple and be humble. Just thank everyone and sit down.

When the master of ceremonies read the names of the Religion and Spirituality recipients, the three winning titles did not include mine. When repeating the names, I listened again more intently, thinking I must have somehow missed it the first time. But, alas, my name wasn't among those announced. Stunned, I felt all the blood draining out of my face as I hypocritically clapped lifelessly for each of the three winning recipients in my category.

Then logic kicked in, and I began to develop misgivings for not entering the "Philosophy" category. Perhaps I had not won because all the book titles in the "Religious and Spirituality" group had titles that usually included syrupy words like beloved, faithfully, heavenly, and so forth. I reasoned, who would the committee have most likely selected to judge these books? Of course, I rationalized, in all probability, they would have chosen people of traditional religions, who might be offended by anything different or unusual. All right, I had defined God as transcending mortal understanding and, consequently, all Western religious philosophies. Indeed, the judges would have been willing to objectify those words—or not.

In the context of consolation, one of my friends reminded me, most great authors are recognized posthumously. This kind of recognition seems to offer small comfort, and for the time being, I shall not anxiously await that recognition, at least not while I'm still alive. I am now writing a book of essays and short stories.

I have come to realize that I have already received a prize before ever entering the contest. I am fortunate to be the recipient of the best award of all, acknowledged collegiality and friendship from my associates. Not an insignificant validation of worth, perhaps a distinction that, in many ways, approaches the significance of the one toward which I initially had striven. However, the most significant reward is that I did it. Eighty percent of the population wants to write a book; less than fifteen percent get it done. The hard work is real, and the flattery is a false illusion. It is a distraction from the actual intent of my writing, which is to alert other people to the essential truth of authenticity each person can find by owning and living their unique truth in life. My manuscripts will continue to flow because I feel driven to express as a writer.

Flattery is usually fraudulent, though often well-intended, it can be excessive and insincere, creating an emotion based on a lie from which you can learn nothing. At it's very worst, flattery pushes you to try to live up to someone else's idea of who or what you should strive to be. My friends and associates have read, understood, and told me it created an effect on them. If that is so, someone's life has become better because they read my book. That is why I write.

# The Lifeguard

IT WAS A COLD WINTER DAY and just turning dusk as my car glided around a bend in the highway. In the few seconds that followed, the whole scenic landscape abruptly changed. It was as if I had suddenly been transported to a different time, utterly alone in a remote place far out in the universe.

The sight of strange yellow lights flickering on the face of a small lake in front of me promoted feelings of apprehension and confusion. The lights projected an evil creation of spirits dancing about on the side of a boathouse located at the far end of the lake. These reflections appeared to arise from beneath the dark water, demanding me to take action! I was confused, unsure of what difference, if any, I could make dealing with creatures from the deep unknown.

It was as if an external force had taken control of me as I parked my car by the side of the road. I sat for a few minutes, bewildered, then cautiously exited the vehicle and strolled toward the lake. During a brief exploration of the area, I found an old rowboat partially hidden nearby. It was as if somebody had placed the boat there in anticipation of my arrival. I quickly surveyed the area but could not detect anything, even remotely human, except a few beer cans tossed irreverently into the weeds.

I firmly pushed the boat through the snow, over crusty ice, and into the cold lake. It seemed to be a natural water body, a primary source, giving life to all the old trees surrounding it. My nerves became calm in response to the life-sustaining powers of the lake.

But as the boat entered the water, I felt repelled by the pungent odor of death arising as a mist from the thick combination of moss and rotten leaves along the shoreline. I wondered if the leaves were a necessary sacrifice sent by the skeleton limbs of cottonwood trees hanging down remorsefully in the water. The trees existed as a metaphor of immortality: death in the winter followed by a grand metamorphosis and return to life the following spring.

When I stepped into the rowboat, it rocked and shuddered as if alive—a cold shiver ran down the length of me. Apprehension about my intended destination became momentarily forgotten when frigid lake water, splashed by my oar, awakened my attention. A fall into the icy water could bring significant hypothermic shock or even drowning.

Boat maintenance suffered from a lack of attention because the craft contained several inches of dirty water. When I looked down, a moonbeam from the partially cloud-hidden moon reflected my face. My reflection stared back through an eerie translucent haze. It appeared as if there was no bottom to the boat. A pretense of support arose from the depth of the lake beckoning to me. It defied the logic of my mind.

My thoughts flashed back to memories of a time when I looked upon the purplish face of a dead man. As a lifeguard, I had pulled him from the lake after his last moment of life had been taken. Resuscitation had proved futile. As I stood up, I noticed a suspicious bruise mark on his forehead, indicating that a speed boat struck his head, inflicting trauma, causing his drowning.

My job as a lifeguard required particular attention because the lake had been roped off and divided into two sections, the smaller area for the swimmers, the more extensive area intended for speed boats and water skiers. The rope was no more than a vain attempt to protect swimmers from water skiers towed by the high-powered speed boats. The skiers showed total disregard to the endangerment created as they buzzed the swimmers who seemed oblivious to the risk of death each time they swam past the ropes into those dangerous waters.

Later, authorities speculated that the drowned swimmer most have, indeed, ventured too far out. No one ever stepped forward to confess a possible "inadvertent mishap." The culprit's confession could never drain that bluish-violet color from the face of the dead man. Nor would the culprit's acceptance of responsibility transfuse color back into the widow's face. Freshness and vitality slowly drained from her life through the combined shock and realization of her beloved partner's death. Her demeanor projected feelings of emptiness, aloneness, and isolation in the vast universe.

Then, my mind returned to the blinking lights in the present. I felt compelled to direct my attention to the situation existing ahead of me as the ascending fog began to swallow the lake and all around it. I could now only see a few feet in front of me and forced to exist in the immediate. As I rowed, I could see my watch, but not the time. During that moment, I realized that visions of time could create distortions in reality.

Light flakes began to fall, and the bottomless boat became an extension of my body. I leaned forward and pulled the oars against the water. Looking down, I realized my reflection had disappeared, no longer found staring back at me in anticipation and fear. How could anyone not wonder, "Have I gone out of my mind? Is this an omen of life lost? My life?"

The snow had stopped, and when I raised my head, I could barely see the ghostly figure of a fox as it ran along the shore. It was so near, yet, as in a dream, so very far from me. Then came the unmistakable sound of a large bird flying above; it could only be sensed, not seen. These creatures did not seem to be moving toward something, but away from it. Every life on earth ends in death, but from the knowledge of this truth emerges a great fear and distraction to humanity, often pushing aside the act of living a life of individual power and dignity.

I was all alone as I moved cautiously across the middle of the lake in a wooden death trap. It seemed more like a coffin than a boat. Fears throughout my life culminated at that moment, gripping me just below the surface of my consciousness. Dread was vaguely perceived, momentarily taken away, as if through the trickster fox's effect of freely running along the shore. This vision then became lost in the sound of the mysterious flying creature whose primary purpose in life seemed only to mock and ridicule my fear.

The fog began to lift, and I could again see the strange lights more clearly. Instinctively, I knew they were calling me. The sight was ghostly.

I paused, took a deep breath, and considered a retreat to the shore from which I had come. I couldn't do it! I had crossed an imaginary line in the middle of the lake, and it would now be farther back than forward.

Then, in response to this logic, the oars boldly stroked the water, pulling me toward my awaiting destiny.

My increased efforts propelled the boat and brought me to the boathouse much quicker than expected. I was startled by a loud thump when the wood boat met the wood deck. I had almost reached the mysterious lights whose flickering reflections seemed to follow me relentlessly as if provoked. These yellow ghosts danced all about the boathouse. They caused me to pause, then struggle to remember why I had come; what surreal calling had brought me here?

After a few minutes, I again resisted a retreat to safety by returning across the lake. I took a deep breath and stepped out of the boat, slowly moved forward, intent on confronting the light's source. I forced myself to take several more steps as I pushed through emotional glue that emanated from past generations of fear. I realized that my lack of movement was a contribution to the continuity of dread. The trip across the lake now seemed like a sprint compared to the next steps I would take.

Then, after a short wait, which seemed like a month or two, I peered around the side of the boathouse. I fully expected an attack by an alien, a ghost, or some other creation of death's mystery, but it wasn't to be. The shocking sight in front of me compelled a retreat, rushing madly across the dock, returning to the vessel from which I had just left. I began rowing with all my might, not in the opposite direction, but toward the source of the lights!

The flashing yellow "spirits" were the turn lights of an automobile that had plunged into the marsh between the back of the boathouse and an old dirt road.

My heart now pumped rapidly, and adrenalin surged throughout my body. When I pulled the oars, I was surprised by the relative ease as the boat moved toward the half-submerged car. I couldn't imagine the water's depth that filled the vehicle, nor could I mentally project the driver's condition.

The marsh now seemed intent on preventing me from reaching its captured prize. But buoyed by humankind's will of mutual survival, I forced the boat next to the car. When I looked through the open window, I could see the dark hair of a motionless woman. There was no sound. I was sure she was dead, so I quietly ventured, "Are you injured?"

From within the vehicle, "Oh, thank God, you heard me calling. My chest hurts, and I am having trouble breathing. The water is cold as ice; I feel like I am slowly freezing to death."

I answered, "It will take just a second or two while I call for help." I quickly punched 911 on my cell phone and informed the operator of the accident. The operator, while staying calm, reassured me, "Responders have been alerted. Help is on the way and will arrive very soon."

I knew the car was sinking, so I refused to risk the woman's life. I needed to get her out of this death trap quickly. Unfortunately, her vehicle had entered the marsh nose-first, and the door became jammed shut by the water's pressure.

I asked her, "Can you move toward me?" She quietly answered, "I can't move very much, but maybe with your help." By working together, she escaped from the automobile. The old boat that seemed like a casket just minutes ago now had become a magnificent life-saving ship. And, given that you ask, yes, our combined weight caused the vessel to dip dangerously deep in the water, but it boldly carried us to the lake shore.

When I lifted her out of the boat, she shivered as she clung tightly to me like a small child to her father. I wondered what she meant when she said she had called out to me. I didn't hear her call, or did I?

She whispered, "Thank you so much for being here! You saved me from death! I gave up hope; I was certain the end was here. I almost stopped believing I would ever hear the sound of another human voice again."

She still shivered from the cold and shock of her ordeal. I choked away the emotion in my throat as I said with considerable masculine bravado requiring no pretense, "There is no way you will die this night!" I covered her with my coat and held her close to me. She could absorb my body heat while we awaited the ambulance. As we waited, I thought about what had happened and what it meant in her life. The very things that frighten us the most often trick us back toward fulfilling individual authenticity and truth. Our lives might otherwise become forgotten and unfinished.

It was impressive when the ambulance arrived so quickly. The demands of its siren pervaded the quiet night. Then the echoing scream of the sheriff's siren followed. The combination of flashing lights jolted my memory to the pulsating yellow turn-lights from the lady's car. I imagined those lights as beautiful spirits beckoning, but they could easily have shorted out and died if not answered immediately by a representative of humankind.

I could only watch as the attendants gently took her from my arms, expertly moving her onto a stretcher and into the ambulance. I felt ashamed when remembering the fear which had smothered and gripped me, but reassured when I turned to take a last look at her car. The yellow lights were no longer visible, having submerged and drowned under the dark water.

Later, a friend informed me that after the ambulance was moving down the road, one of the attendants tried to check their patient's blood pressure. When it didn't register as desired, the attendant response was loud, as if the patient wasn't in attendance, "I'm not getting a good reading on her blood pressure!"

Despite her physical problems, but happy to be alive, the patient asked as if being severe, "Oh my, I do hope that doesn't mean that I'm dead?"

The senior attendant completely missed the woman's intended humor and responded somewhat indignantly, "No, of course, you're not dead, you are just suffering from shock. We will get an accurate reading as soon as you warm up."

The attendants were again surprised by their patient's next statement, "You know, I feel so sad because I didn't think to ask that good fellow his name. Now he may never receive due recognition. You know, he did take a great risk when saving my life. I wonder how many other people drove by the lake tonight? But that doesn't matter; I will remember him for the rest of my life."

As they moved away, I began shivering from the cold moisture absorbed in my shirt when holding her close to me. My coat was also damp, but I couldn't suppress a slight smile of satisfaction as I began to row that fantastic old boat back across the lake toward my car. It was then that it occurred to me; I hadn't thought to ask the woman her name. But, I reasoned, it doesn't matter, we will probably never meet again—but I will always remember her as long as I am alive.

# Cinnamon Rolls

When I was a young lad, my family didn't go to church—at least not in the usual way. Our place of worship had no walls. Instead, it existed as a dream filled with gold rewards, adventures with Zorro, and sacred cinnamon rolls. There was never the waxy smell of burning candles, nor the sweet scent of flowers in tribute to otherworldly stuff. The ritual was always the heavenly experience of freshly baked feelings shared in a living celebration of life. We had this perfect thing: childhood innocence.

Mom would sometimes teasingly say, "I feel like having one of the Little Bakery's cinnamon rolls." My brother and I would look at each other smiling, as we enthusiastically agreed, "Hey, mom, me too, yummy."

It was always the first thing in the morning, and we would be wearing our faded cotton cowboy pajamas. They were still warm and comfortable after having just returned from last night's adventures in dreams. It may seem that cowboy pajamas might be in contradiction to the nighttime dreamland, where I was gallantly fighting with swords at the side of Zorro. Naturally, he would never have been caught dead with anyone wearing such apparel. But he ignored my battle armaments in tribute to all heroic dreams. Of course, we won our valiant battle against evil, besting the banditos and making them look quite inept in the process. If you happen to be a bad guy, be warned, never turn your back on Zorro because you might soon find the letter Z carved on your backside!

This morning, there was no time for arguments with my brother about whose turn it was to go to the store. We hurried to get dressed because we both felt compelled to get the bakery while the rolls were still warm and fresh after being removed from the oven. We pleaded out loud at each other, "Please, don't let them all be gone!" One time in the past, they had disappeared with a hungry buyer before we rushed into the bakery a little later than usual.

We quickly finished dressing, and as if members of a track relay team, we were ready to be handed the baton. Mom was waiting to hand off the money she held in her hand. She always seemed to know how much cash we would need, and as our team captain, she symbolically admonished, "Don't lose the change, bring it back here to me!"

We raced out the door and down the street. Moments later, we stood in front of the bakery. The window invited us with all sorts of fantastic delights, but our eyes could only see the light brown rolls with white frosting waiting in a metal pan. Not one of the batch was gone, but we kept close guard, considering our previous experience in which some competitors appeared from nowhere and whisked our prize away.

Upon entering the store, it was as if we had walked into a holy sanctuary. But there weren't any flowers on an altar, nor incense and candles burning tribute to some mysterious deity. Instead, the only pungent smell experienced was cinnamon and freshly baked bread. All the other scents, imagined or real, just seemed to fade away.

Breathing heavily from our sprint, we would jointly tell the bakery lady of our sacred quest. She always smiled as she happily announced, "Good timing, boys, we only took the rolls out of the oven a few minutes ago!"

The ritual began as we watched her use a spatula to lift them gently from the pan. These delicacies were so soft they could easily tear apart and float away if not handled with care. We felt like participants in holy communion. But what she held could never be confused as unleavened bread. We observed with devout attention as she put a half dozen rolls into a white "Little Bakery" sack. They were thick with cinnamon and juicy raisins.

We handed our monetary "offering" to the priestess, who responded with a loving smile. She said, "Thank you!" as she looked into our eyes and shared in our happiness and excitement. I wanted to invite her to come and share with us, but we paused just long enough to repeat, "Thank you!" before darting out the door.

It was my brother who, with a certain air of authority, had carefully taken the sack and twelve cents in change from her because, as he would often remind me, he was my elder by eighteen months. I didn't argue because he did seem much older and bigger than me.

While hurrying toward home, our pace changed to an efficient, but fast, walk because of our delicate cargo. We paused only once to open the sack and quickly view the contents. The paper bag rattled as my brother pushed it under my nose. I could feel the streaming heat moving the thick scent of cinnamon and goodness into the center of my being. It was only through the fear of fingerprints that we were able to muster the sufficient restraint required to keep from brushing our fingers across the warm frosting. My mouth was salivating as we hurried up the street, and when quickly swallowing, I could taste the cinnamon roll as if I had just devoured it.

In anticipation of our arrival home to the relay finish point, Mom already had her coffee poured and mixed with cream and sugar. She had also poured two glasses of cold milk for us. We quickly pulled three chairs out from around the table and eagerly leaned forward. Mom carefully opened the sack and looked inside. I could feel a thrill of happiness deep within my stomach. I smiled in anticipation as she withdrew her hand from the bag and carefully handed us each a roll.

The frosting stuck to my fingers as I wolfed down the first mouth full calming my excitement and expectation. During our roll-fest, I didn't taste any of the ingredients as separate from the whole product. They combined to create something unique. Our baby brother was sound asleep in his crib, but he would join our celebration of life in a couple of years. Although working in another town, our dad was there with us, too, although only in spirit. I know this to be true because I thought of him driving down the highway toward his customers in the next town. He once told me he had found all the restaurants with the best pie.

We were always cautious about finishing our first roll together because the race was now over. Eating faster than the others meant you had to sit and watch until they also polished off their first one. I drank some of the cold milk and strategically swallowed my last bit as Mom handed each of us our second roll. I smiled when Mom licked the warm frosting off her fingers before picking up her coffee cup and taking another sip. There was a sacred feeling of unity that morning, while we were all sharing, my mother, my brother, and me.

After finishing with my second roll, I savored the lingering taste before drinking the last of my milk. I looked over at my brother as he picked up a plump raisin he had purposely dropped on the table in front of his half-empty glass. He popped the morsel into his mouth and acted as if it were the last bit of fruit of its kind in the world. I could see him watching me out of the corner of his eye. I felt happy for my brother and my mom, but most of all, I felt a warmth flowing from deep within myself. I didn't know then that what I was feeling was love, but I know now that the cinnamon rolls couldn't have tasted the same had we not been sharing them. And as for the meaning of the plump raisin my brother mockingly ate, as is the ways of many older siblings, he had assumed the tremendous responsibility of carrying the sack home to the finish line where we celebrated our victory together. These rituals were the links that bound us together.

I now wonder, did the Zorro in my dream look suspiciously like my brother? How could anybody know? Zorro is perfect. But throughout the nightly adventures, a mask hid his real identity. However, there existed a dichotomy in my relationship with my brother. He was my hero and sometimes even my friend, but there has also been a fierce battle of siblings. As the firstborn, he tried to remain aloof throughout his life until the end. I displayed the other side of our rivalry, always trying to measure up, or in other words, become a significant force. We were growing apart in good and bad ways. These were the kind of experiences that continually shaped our lives.

I wanted my brother to stop badgering me with his persistent claim of superiority over me. I desired his encouragement or even his recognition of our contrasting individuality and true-selves. I wanted a best friend, a Zorro, with whom I could join in the adventures of life. As we grew older, this quality slowly became lost in all the games played.

Many years later, shortly before his death, my brother told me he had left me out of his will. He went on to say that as far back as he could remember, he had always liked to hurt me. When I asked, "Why?" he could only answer that he didn't know. Later, I concluded that my brother lost his status in existence as number one in our parent's eyes from the moment of my birth.

After his confession, he pulled from a tin box five thousand dollars, which he held out to me in one hand. Within his other hand, he clutched an additional five thousand dollars in one-hundred-dollar bills, which he then slowly returned to the box full of money as he declared, "Money means nothing to me!"

During his whole life, he had been miserly, unsharing, and often hurtful. Even during his moment of generosity, he hadn't changed when seemingly giving as an expression of caring. But I know my brother had a love for me, mostly as exhibited through inadvertent happenings such as a plump raisin rolling out on the kitchen table. In the end, it was all excellent, and he was who he was: a blend of different ingredients mixed, then shared with love in the celebration of life.

My family existed in a physical, mental, and spiritual cathedral called life. The love we often experienced seemed imperfect, undefined, and sometimes unrecognized, but I assure you, our feelings were real.

My older brother usually didn't recognize, honor, or encourage me in acknowledgment of my search for freedom. As I ponder this, the following question crashes through my mind, "If I had been born first, would I have been as my brother, and he as me?"

Carved in 800 B.C. on the Greek temple of Delphi are three words. "Know thy self."

# Freedom

MY FATHER ALWAYS seemed upbeat and positive, but conclusions assumed from observing other people's outward demeanor are not a reliable basis for assessing an individual's real mood. The truth of this possible contradiction was established in my mind early in my teens when my brother brought home a recorded rendition of Arthur Miller's play, *Death of a Salesman.*

Our family gathered together that warm summer evening, not knowing we would soon be listening to the recording. Mom's voice called our family to the front room, an area always reserved for special events like holidays. The excitement began to increase when she said, "Robert is back from the record shop with a surprise. He will get it going in a few minutes. So, come on in here, guys; you won't need tickets for this show." Then she announced the play's name, about which none of us knew anything at the time.

The following few minutes were a bit hectic as we found our usual seats and settled back to enjoy the play. Suddenly during the presentation, our father could no longer endure the sadness projected by the story's protagonist, Willy, the salesman. As our dad (a salesman like Willy) later explained, "It was not that I was much like Willy; it was that I was merely too closely related to his own life experiences." Oh, I surmised, so Dad is like Willy.

Dad coughed in a futile attempt to silence a sob erupting from the depth of his soul as he quickly abandoned the family group that night.

He had suffered much of his own life through unhappiness, as expressed in the play. It had exposed complex emotions he had suppressed for far too many years. It was the only time I ever saw my father cry. I do not doubt that experiencing the release of suppressed emotion can bring significant confusion to any of us during our lives.

Four of us remained to experience the play, which had temporarily been placed on pause by Robert. "I'm turning the machine back on," he said while looking toward Mom to approve his decision. There were no more interruptions to our evening. By the time the last act of the play ended, my little brother had fallen asleep, which seemed to bring our day to an end. However, scenes from the production were renewed in my dreams that night, especially when my father became upset. I could understand the pain he felt, but not the reason.

During that period of my life, I worked as an orderly at the hospital. Many times when I came home late at night, Dad would be sitting in the kitchen, both his elbows pressed on the table  His arms and hands supported his head, and he usually dropped off to sleep in this manner. In the winter, the heat-blasted from the kitchen oven engulfing everything like hell-fire from a flame thrower.

The room filled with clouds of cigarette smoke wafting continuously from slow dying cigarette butts cluttered and smoldering in a large, conveniently placed, ashtray. Perhaps the smoke was intended to obscure memories of dying dreams, plans, and hopes, like the remnants of a previous nightmare, suppressed and partially forgotten the following morning.

Burn marks on the table and floor were glaring reminders of the hot ash and the cigarette butts, which dropped out of the ashtray after losing balance. No one ever seemed to question this possible fire source that could burn down the house one night.

Sitting on the table next to the ashtray was a bottle of spirits and a half-full drinking glass. Ringlets of moisture crept slowly down the outside of the drinking glass, pretending to water the yellow painted flowers camouflaging the container and its contents, maybe concealing something promising the relief of pain.

Before the relatively inexpensive advent of television as a primary entertainment source before the 1950s, bar-hopping was a common means of distraction for American households' adult members. This accomplishment manifested through the activity of one or more persons having a couple of drinks in a bar. They then moved on to another bar, and so on, visiting with friends and acquaintances. This activity usually reflected the same repetitious conversations and jokes shared during earlier visits at other lounges.

Because dad was an insurance salesman in that area of the city, he had a business relationship with many of these people. He rationalized that drinking with them in this manner was necessary for the success of his job. His rationale would have seemed somewhat more reasonable if a monetary return justified the many hours he and my mother spent in bars. Combine that with the modest pay he received from his hours on the job, and it could not be considered a fair trade-off.

Both he and my mother would often come home "high," as they liked to call it, and they sometimes seemed happy, but as the high wore off, so did the happiness. Mom would go to bed, leaving Dad sitting at the kitchen table smoking and drinking one last drink. I wondered later if drinking was a pretense of happiness by people who, in this manner, anesthetized their minds from the confusing pain of living lives of desperate futility.

Upon arising the following day, I had no conscious awareness of second-hand smoke's rancid smell, yet that smell still repels me. Every morning my dad would wake from sleep showing no adverse signs of the previous night's activities. He dressed in a suit and tie, "You need to look sharp!" he enthusiastically said with pride as he looked at his wristwatch. Every time he started through the door to leave the house, he seemed to know just where in his territory he needed to be to sell insurance or collect amounts due from customers.

He usually walked his route, greeting with a happy salutation every person he met along the way, a client, or anybody else. In the evening, he shared his experiences of the day with my brothers and me. I suspect it was his fatherly manner of mentoring us while at the same time reminding himself of that day's activities. He told me that I am a natural salesman, so selling is the type of work I should do when I graduate. It was not what I pictured myself doing, so I did not respond.

One day he talked about having a brief conversation with a man named Ralph. He always asked Ralph a rhetorical question such as, "How are you doing, Ralph?" Ralph responded with sad information about his usual physical complaint, which only varied slightly from day to day and month to month, "Not so good, Mark, my ankle (or knee or stomach or head) has been bothering me."

A week or two later, when my father came home for lunch, he said, "Ralph proved himself right, it turned out he was not so good; I found out that he died yesterday. The doctor was not sure of what caused it." The implication here was Ralph brought it on himself through negative thinking and self-perpetuated pity. "He died from boredom. But on second thought, he had probably given up on his life long ago when his wife left him," Dad said.

I wondered to myself if Ralph ever went bar-hopping because it seemed to me that many of the people in bars focus on various forms of self-pity, much of the time. These same people were always the victims of someone or something: "I just can't catch a break, or, if it weren't for bad luck, I wouldn't have any luck at all."

When my brothers and I were very young, our parents were often away from home on the forays of bar-hopping. However, we sometimes needed our mother and father's attention to give us a sense of direction, the gift of purpose, and some boundaries to help create a deeper meaning in our lives. Perhaps we expressed a milder form of self-pity when we sometimes acted out our anger doing foolish and mischievous things without realizing why.

In return for their inattention, when we were about ten years old, we punished our parents in various ways (of which they had no awareness) like when we ran away from home. However, it never seemed to my older brother and me that we were inflicting punishment on anybody in any manner. However, the hidden penalty was the intent directed by the denial of our presence.

This particular time, we walked with purpose in a southerly direction down railroad tracks leading to the magical, far-away Black Forest where we planned to live off the land. Our inspiration came by way of *Tarzan of the Apes* movies in which he was adopted, raised, and cared for by apes. We knew there were no animals such as this in the Black Forest who might care for us, but we thought we could bag deer with bow and arrow (if, incidentally, we had a bow and those deadly projectiles). We could also learn to throw a hunting knife into the flesh of stalking lions or bears with deadly accuracy. (You may have already surmised, we also didn't have a hunting knife.) How cool that would be, sitting around a campfire eating the meat of wild animals, maybe something like eating s'mores or toasted marshmallows on the end of a stick.

Because we had often climbed trees during our youth, we felt convinced we could sleep in trees high above the ground, safe from animals. We gave no thought to potential falls from trees or to the cold Colorado winters. After all, Tarzan never had any problem coping with snow in the jungle. Preparation, it seemed, was only a matter of imagination and enthusiasm bonded by conviction.

As we meandered along the train tracks, we found Indian chalk (so-called), a hard rock from which we managed to get a few marks of color on our faces without breaking our skin. I didn't think my brother looked particularly savage, and he repaid my observation by not paying any more attention to my menacing demeanor than he usually did. "Stand back or lose your scalp, white man," said I while detecting a hint of fear crossing his face. Robert answered, "I think I need to find a place to go to the bathroom." Disappointed, I waited patiently. Then we moved on, expecting to reach our destination before dark.

While surveying the terrain for wild animal sightings, we spotted a sandpit in which we previously had gone swimming. Without exchanging as much as a word, we found ourselves moving in unison directly toward the water where crawdads, snakes, and lizards sometimes could be seen along the shore.

We talked enthusiastically, each sharing gifts from our imagination, yet refusing to acknowledge that we had probably missed by several millennium seeing dinosaurs, woolly mammoths, and saber-toothed tigers. Of course, we never mentioned to each other that the present absence of these beasts carried no immediate personal disappointment.

We conducted a brief search around the water but found nothing of interest, not even a crawdad. The sun was hot, so when my older brother began to strip down, I joined him, and we quickly became content to delay our trip to the Black Forest and, instead, take a dip in the refreshing water of the sandpit. We had no modesty as we stripped and carefully placed our clothes where we hoped there were no ants. Robert had no reason to warn me about ants, but I responded while rubbing my backside, "Thanks, but it would have been better had you told me this the last time we were here."

An old log floated nearby like a menacing crocodile, but this image immediately transformed through creative imagination into a luxury liner. Permission to come aboard? However, Peg-leg Jim and One-ear Robert are not to be bound by such requirements. We boarded that seaworthy transportation, and as we pushed away from the shore, a red-winged blackbird rose in fright from a nearby bush. Our shared alarm and apprehension were at least equal to that of the small bird, but we quickly realized the noise was not a deadly attack by the giant prehistoric flying reptile about which we had talked earlier that day.

We laughed and made squawking sounds while flapped our arms (somewhat like a bird might do) as we floated a few yards out from the shore. Momentarily losing my balance should have been a reminder that I didn't know how to swim (I did a weak dog crawl), but because my brother (like Tarzan) was a good swimmer, I was not concerned with my deficiency of talent.

Later, when I accidentally fell into the water, my brother quickly pulled me back onto the log—my escape from danger followed with rippled feelings of fear. We spoke without words; the rescue was just what brothers do, like fighting with each other. After releasing our emotions, we occupied ourselves doing something else as if the recovery (or a fight) had never occurred. Coincidentally, a few years later, we both held summer jobs as lifeguards. That was when our lives started to drift apart, each of us going his own way.

We languished on that log with our bodies exposed to the rays of the sun for most of the day, but later, as quickly as we had entered the water, the natural G.P.S. of our minds (and hunger) dictated to us that it was now time to return home.

The fun we had that day quickly became forgotten as we gingerly slipped into our clothes. We became painfully aware of the sun's magnified heat's damaging effect, which reflected off the water. When we arrived home, our mother took one glance at our sunburned faces and said nothing, communicating without using words, which is a Mother's way.

Mom reminded me that she and I were going to the movies; my brother was going to a Boy Scout meeting. Earlier, my brother and I put vinegar all over our bodies because it was supposed to stop the burning gift from the sun. But our bodies itched, and we smelled like dinner salads.

After dinner, Mom strategically laid out my shirt and a pair of wool pants. She instructed me to get dressed for the movie. I looked at the wool pants with disdain, but carefully put them on.

The theater was within walking distance, and I moved very gingerly, trying to walk stiffly without touching my clothes to my body. It didn't work! The sun disappearing behind the mountains to the west had tattooed reminders of its fire all over my body. I thought to myself, "Moms are usually good to have around, but sometimes they can be kind of mean. It was as if she thought that by requiring me to wear wool pants would teach me a lesson. Ha! I was no pushover. It was like telling Tarzan not to swing in trees because he might get a splinter.

That night at the movies, the theater management was giving away a basket of groceries. When chosen, and invited with other young fellows to the stage, any young boy will take part in an undisclosed competition to determine the winner and a prize for winning the contest. At my mother's urging to stand up, and after being selected, I painfully made my way to the stage with the other eight guys.

Ushers brought tables out, one for each of us. (So far, the ordeal didn't seem to be too bad.) At the same time, they now put safety pins and diapers on top of the tables. Then dolls were brought out, which, a man with a microphone explained, were the competition source. It was a race to see which boy would be the fastest to change his doll's diaper: safety pins and diapers now conveniently placed next to pretend babies. People in the audience began to laugh at the sight of bewilderment expressed on these future fathers' faces, these expert diaper-changers.

When the man in charge yelled, "Go!" It all became a blur in my mind, but I became strategically guided by the memory of my mother putting a diaper on my little brother when he was a baby. I fumbled around and in my haste, stuck my finger, and dropped the pins once or twice while trying to get the diaper to hold still, but just as it seemed that I had got the job done, the man yelled again, but this time he said, "Stop!"

While holding up the winner's doll, the diaper dropped off, and the audience screamed in laughter. I was confused and embarrassed; even the miniature Dora must have wanted to cover herself.

As my mother and I made our way home, she said, "You did well; I am proud of you." And I was proud too. I had practically forgotten the hell from my sunburn as I carried the groceries toward home. I hoped my father would be sitting at the kitchen table when we walked in with the prize. I wanted him to be happy, and he did seem pleased as he complimented me on my victory.

Later that night, as I passed through the kitchen, I could see he had dropped off to sleep with his head supported by his hands. This form of denial was his reflection of the society where we lived where one may view a significant proportion of the population in much the same passive way. Somehow we have been conditioned to inaction by such words as, "You can't fight city hall!"

Once while playing in our back yard, two young girls walked by and nastily declared, "White trash!" At first, my brother and I were confused by this declaration from these two girls we had never seen before. We wondered where they had learned such mean, vindictive words.

Who or what might have prompted the girls to feel such contempt toward strangers? We looked at each other and laughed at their anger and arrogant attitude as they continued down the alley with their noses upturned like trained seals at the zoo.

In retrospect, my brother and I almost always received significant freedom. We roamed outside the confines of controlling parents who condition their children like robots by repeating the same repetitive lessons taught to them by the same unfulfilled role models who taught them during their childhood.

We undoubtedly were viewed as rebels and rejected by the fear-inspired values of the traditional establishment. In accord with some religions, we were bound for hell and damnation. Is it not interesting how freedom is one person's hell, but ofttimes another person's heaven?

*I think I could turn and live with animals,*
*Not one kneels to another,*
*nor to his kind that lived*
*Thousands of years ago.*
*Not one is responsible or unhappy*
*over the whole Earth.*

—Walt Whitman, *Leaves of Grass: The Death-Bed Edition.*

# The Ordeal

ON THE WAY HOME from his first day of school, a small boy named Joey entered a grocery store, and just inside the front entrance, he spotted a candy machine. Looking into the device through a glass viewing window, he could see colorfully wrapped candy all positioned to create desire. Like magic, the boy felt instantly drawn under the spell of that evil vending machine.

As Joey stood there, he could feel his mouth salivating at the possibility of sweetness exciting his taste buds. Chocolate had been his favorite during his whole life (now six years), and there within his reach was his first choice of all the different kinds of temptations. He thought to himself that it just wasn't fair to tempt him like this; after all, he was just a small boy with no money to pay for such lavish things. The truth be told, he had no money to pay for anything after quickly spending his allowance moments after his dad handed it to him yesterday. (Oh, destitution, spare me thy curse.)

Then he became inspired. Without further contemplation, Joey reached his hand up through the slot intended for the ejection of candy bars in response to money deposited into the machine. At first, he didn't think he could reach the candy, but with a little adjustment, his hand finally clutched the object of his desire. He then realized that he couldn't get his hand out of the machine, so Joey began to cry and carry on as if the dispenser had reached out and grabbed his hand during a fateful moment when he wasn't looking.

Responding to Joey's cries, women ran to his aid but fainted when they saw the machine eating his hand. Then men from around the store hurried to help him, but they also began to faint. When the women started to recover, they tried to instruct him on how to escape from his ordeal, but to no avail.

At the very instant, when everyone had given up, an older white-bearded black man entered the store, walked up to the small boy, and said quietly, "If you want to get your hand out of the machine, you must first let go of the candy. The boy stopped crying and looked at him in wonder. Slowly his fingers began to release the candy, and his hand slid quickly out of the machine. Joey examined his small hand and finding no "bite" marks, he paused long enough to take a last look at the candy, then darted out the door and was free again. And all the people applauded the white-bearded man for presenting Joey with an escape from the machine.

The moral to the story: Anybody who has ever struggled soon learns the price of that which we hope to obtain.

# A Symbol

EARLY ONE SPRING DAY, an elementary school teacher explained to her class about the four seasons: spring, summer, fall, and winter. She said that each season is composed of three months. Because the present time of the year was spring, her lesson's focus was on spring symbols.

The teacher told the class how the native people in South America identified the four seasons by solstices and equinoxes. Their calendar reflects activities such as hunting, fishing, planting, harvesting, and religious rituals. She also talked about other things, including the birth of plant and animal life, renewal, re-growth, and even resurrection, as expressed by symbols and interpretations in some scientific and religious doctrines.

As if the children needed reminding, she told them that this was the time of year Easter was celebrated, and they immediately became intensively involved. They enthusiastically talked about the symbolic meaning of Easter eggs, chocolate bunny rabbits, and little yellow marshmallow chicks used to decorate and fill Easter baskets. However, she knew that a bit more attention to comparing these symbolic eatables might be required to meet her lesson's intent.

Even though the children seemed to understand her explanation of facts such as she used in describing the customs of native peoples, the teacher wanted them to have a broader, more lasting understanding of symbols through the eyes of their own experience. She wasn't sure how she would accomplish this goal but was confident she could make it happen.

That evening after school, while shopping at a local supermarket, the teacher spotted some plastic eggs used in a pantyhose display by a line called L'eggs. Almost immediately, she knew this was the answer to her dilemma about getting her class more involved. She told the grocer why she wanted the plastic eggs and asked if he would sell them. But, rather than sell them, the grocer happily gave them to her as he said, "You can just go ahead and take them for the kids; I was going to put this display in the trash anyway."

In the class was a student named Steven, who had experienced many health problems during two dark years of illness. This distraction had held him below the level of academic progress expected from children at his grade level. He hadn't been able to keep up because of repeated absences, so it had been decided after consideration by the school principal and Steven's parents to remain at his present grade level. "It is for his benefit," they rationalized. However, this strategy overlooked one significant problem; Steven was already more than a head taller than the other children in his class. Sometimes being cruel, children frequently teased him through rejection and verbal abuse, but Steven always remained patient with them.

It was Friday when the teacher passed out the plastic eggs, one for each child. She instructed them to think about their egg over the weekend and, after coloring the egg's exterior, place something in it, which would symbolize the meaning of Easter eggs and other such goodies.

Upon returning to school that following Monday, the children placed their eggs, all having been colorfully decorated, on the teacher's desk. After checking the class attendance and finding all the students present, the teacher began to open each egg one at a time to share the contents with these future artists of the world.

The first egg she opened contained a flower. The teacher exclaimed, "What a good symbol the flower is. Flowers express love, and we also use flowers at funerals to symbolize the rebirth of life. A little girl proudly said, "That's my egg, teacher." The teacher acknowledged her saying, "What a good job you have done, Jeannie."

The next egg she picked up felt heavy, and when she opened it up, she found a rock. She thought to herself, "This is Sammie's egg; he just didn't understand the assignment." Then she pushed that egg over to the side of her desk and reached for another egg. But Sammie was now waving his hand to be recognized. The teacher said, "Yes, Sammie, what is it?" Then, Sammie anxiously questioned her, "Why did you push my egg to the side of your desk?" When she told him all she found was a rock, he asked her to turn the stone over. When she did as he asked, she could see moss on the underside of the stone. "That is wonderful," she said in surprise; the moss symbolizes the existence of life, even when it appears to be gone. Good job, terrific, Sammie!"

She opened the next egg, and out flew a beautiful butterfly. "Oh, that is so good; the caterpillar transforms into another form, a beautiful butterfly." The teacher did not have to ask whose egg they were looking at; she could see Gina's face glowing with pride. "Good job, Gina."

The teacher opened the next egg, where she found nothing; it was empty. Of course, she knew right away; it was Steven's egg. She thought to herself, "Even though Steven is the biggest and oldest kid in the class, he just can't manage to do anything right." She then pushed his egg over to the side of her desk. This time, Steven waved his hand, and when she called on him, he asked why she had pushed his egg to the side. She patiently explained to him that it was empty. He retorted, "So was Christ's tomb, and that was religion's symbol of his resurrection into life. But my dad is a scientist, and we have faith in the Big Bang theory. Dad says because neither one of these theories has absolute proof, we must respect other people's beliefs.

Two weeks before Easter, Steven died. His teacher and classmates attended the funeral. Steven's grieving Mother and Father watched as the children each, in turn, placed a colorful plastic egg on the top of the small casket. All the plastic eggs were empty but two. The first of these contained a toy rocket ship. The other egg held a little yellow marshmallow chicken; its head had been bitten and presumably eaten. Close examination disclosed a child's tooth-marks, proving that a hungry child had severed the head of the pastel delicacy. Someone suggested the child might have eaten the chicken's head in tribute to Steven, no longer there to eat it himself. Another person guessed that the small rocket ship represented science. However, Steven's father said that this story proves nothing more than humankind's increased consumption of sweets during periods of the equinox.

# The Cave

I WANDERED THROUGH New York City; I had no money; my only possession was the white Navy uniform I was wearing. You might wonder how I had come to find myself experiencing such undesirable circumstances. I accepted the risk of going A.W.O.L. when confronted with the intended theft of my freedom and self-esteem by representatives of the Navy. They planned to teach me a lesson through the process of military discipline. The complete story requires returning a few months earlier when I was still a high school student.

In response to the conflict in Korea, and the lack of volunteers to serve in the military, the U.S. government established mandatory registration for the draft. A senior in high school could opt-out of the selection by joining a reserve unit of any military service branch, which was why I reluctantly joined the Navy Reserve. Also, I choose the Navy because the uniform appeared unique and seldom seen in our inland city. However, activation would not occur if the qualified person remained in school. It became essential to continue an academic journey, even if for no other reason than to avoid the draft and the consequent activation. The significance of the war had nothing to do with my life, or so I thought.

Comprising a school's student body are individuals who break into different groups or categories. I was a jock; that is to say, an athlete, and, ultimately, considered to be a star swimmer. As a swimmer during each of the three years of high school, I achieved all-city, all-state honors, and our team was also all-city and all-state during those years. In my senior year, I was co-captain of the group. There were times I pretended to be unaware of the prestige experienced, but my decorated letter sweater represented a blatant denial of my false modesty.

Things were unfolding pretty well in my life, mainly when I learned that two regional universities would be offering me an athletic scholarship to their respective schools in my senior year. Because of a lack of resources, I had not given much thought to the prospect of attending college, but the idea now became desirable. The word of the athletic awards leaked out from one of the universities because a prominent fraternity planned to have a party honoring elite athletes to their school. Of course, the event intended to gain the prestige of future sport-stars joining their group. It was a pleasant surprise when I received a message inviting me to attend the party. My girlfriend, the first love in my life, became just as excited and impressed when I told her the two of us would be going to the party. We both thought it would be cool, a feather in my cap if I belonged to a fraternity.

It was a wild party, way beyond my limited experience with such things. The drinking and wildness buried me. I was totally out of my comfort zone but carried forward by the surging tide of my many new (potential) friends with their booming voices and attempts at one-upsmanship. By the end of the party, I felt delusional, confused, utterly inadequate, and unfit for fraternity life. Consequently, I assumed that the chaos I experienced might somehow reflect the nature of university life.

Upon returning to school the following week, and having lost sense of my life's direction, I started skipping classes for no apparent reason or justification. I was kicked out of school a few weeks later for ditching, and also, as a result of my usual average grades that had, consequent to my lack of attendance, dropped dramatically. Sometimes choices are not made consciously, but we are still held responsible for the outcome.

I enrolled in another school intended for dropouts and other people, such as myself. Entering this new environment, ironically, soon gave me a much higher sense of fulfillment and purpose. Luckily, I only needed a few credits to graduate, one of which was chemistry. The chemistry teacher was outstanding, and without question, she was the primary person who helped me become emotionally resurrected Consequently, I started doing much better. I was the only student in her class, and she was very generous to me with her time. She assured me that my intellect was excellent, as proven by my completion of some Oxidation-Reduction problems. For beginners in chemistry, these calculations are long and considered an extreme challenge. Sometimes lacking the time required for completion, I left them incomplete at the end of class. I returned and continued to solve them the following day. My teacher helped build my self-confidence by convincing me that because I remembered my place in the problem and picked it up with such ease, it was proof of a keen mind. Frequently we would talk during much of the designated class time about life, and we each shared our projections about the future of human existence. I now looked forward to the daily attendance of being at my new school.

Unfortunately, having been expelled from the previous school activated my eligibility for duty in the Navy Reserve. It happened somewhat rapidly. Though I was not pleased with most of my choices during the prior few months, they were now history, and I only had myself to blame. However, I now managed to fulfill the requirements needed to graduate from high school.

A few weeks later, activated in the Navy, I found myself in boot camp at the Great Lakes Naval Training Base. I started to get into the swing of things and designated the (honorary) athletic petty officer for my boxing, rope climbing, and swimming skills. When the naval base announced a swimming meet for the entire 9th district, I reveled in the chance to show off my skills, and perhaps, if things went well, possibly land a sports instructor position or something of that sort at the base. As it turned out, I swam against swimmers who had been competitors in the Olympics. Fortunately, I won my events and awarded three first-place trophies.

Oh yes, it seemed that I was a big deal in our training unit. So, somewhat in response to my lofty status, when I got into a battle with another sailor during a work assignment, I felt compelled to set things straight as if it were my duty after he tried to knee me in the groin. I hit him only once, and he yelled in pain and held his hands to his newly broken jaw. My reputation now seemed justly appeased, so I returned to my barracks, not knowing the extent of his injury. It was a freak accident in which harm to that degree was certainly never my intent.

Almost immediately, with no questions asked, and no chance to tell my side of the incident, the Navy quickly transferred me to an aircraft carrier dry-docked in the Brooklyn Navy Yard. Upon my arrival, a Navy person assigned a cot to me in a sleeping area where approximately ten other men also had their accommodations. Each man had a locker nearby in which to store his things. I was puzzled when these men seemed to withdraw and avoid interacting with me from the moment I entered my new quarters.

The following morning a sailor in charge directed me to a job. While experiencing the assignment, I soon realized that the post's intent would be a part of a plan to teach me a military discipline lesson. During the next several days, my job consisted of chipping paint in transformer holes below deck where the noise, heat, and dust were stifling. More than the work itself, the loud generator sound created a particular problem for me because my work during the previous summer had been to operate an extremely noisy hose-braiding machine in a manufacturing plant. I experienced hearing deficiencies due to that job. Now, the environment in which I chipped paint created an increasingly more significant problem with my hearing from the first day forward.

As my hearing got progressively worse, I became shunned an even greater extent by the other sailors who, I believed, were instructed to do so. Depression started to take hold of me, but I resigned to make the best of it. Then, one night after completing my work, I was pleased that the day was finally over. Without bothering to think of anything else, I left my electric shaver on my bunk while taking a quick shower. When I returned to my cot, the shaver was missing. I inquired who it was that had taken my property, but no one would answer. The men just sat looking at me as if their silence advised me that I should have known better than to leave anything unattended and not placed in my assigned locker. We were told never to leave anything out of our physical presence in boot camp, such as objects like my electric razor left lying on the bed. I felt angry at myself for such a dumb mistake that would only aggravate my present miserable situation.

The Navy had already labeled me a trouble-maker. However, I now felt a bit like a leper shamed for dropping his index finger here, a big toe there, or even while eating his dinner, observe part of his nose disengage, then fall and disappear into a bowl of hot tomato soup.

Feelings of rejection, anger, and shame drove me to finish dressing and exit from the sleeping area. I blindly followed various unfamiliar passageways leading up through the ship and finally to the flight deck. I stepped out, paused, and took a deep breath of fresh air. Only one light flickered dimly from an office in the super-deck above, so I stayed in the dark, where the stars could be seen bright and abundant. I remembered observing those same stars high above the mountains back in my home state of Colorado. For the first time in weeks, feelings of independence and freedom were returning to me.

As my eyes continued adjusting to the darkness of night, I could discern the vague shape of a metal scaffolding that arose about three or four stories above the ground below and adjacent to the ship. The skeleton-like structure intends civilian workers to remodel the ship's superstructure during the daylight hours.

Perhaps I already knew, even while ascending the stairs and passageways leading to the ship's deck, that I was rejecting and consequently stopping what I considered the unfair abuse I had been experiencing. Then, without another thought, I stepped into the darkness and slowly descended, climbing down the scaffolding to the dock below.

I had no idea where I would go, nor any notion of a means for survival as I cautiously made my way through the shadows of the shipyard to a gate guarded by an M.P. (military police). Extending from either side of the gate was a fifteen-foot-high wire fence blocking my escape to Brooklyn and freedom. Only then did I wonder about the action I had chosen. However, whether or not my response was justifiable in the military or society's eyes seemed unimportant. The treatment was unacceptable as far as my background was concerned. During my life, I lived freely, generally existing as I pleased without strangers telling me who or what I should be.

After making my way to the gate, I lay hidden under a nearby pine tree's branches. It took a significant amount of time and patience to determine the requirements of escape. By observing and calculating the traffic on the outside of the gate, I finally developed a solution to the obstacle blocking me. Every third time the traffic light changed, two buses would arrive simultaneously from opposite directions, one on each street side. People who exited the bus from the outer area crossed the road, adding to the crowd debarking from the bus already at the gate. I calculated the M.P. would be distracted; this would be my only opportunity to escape.

The timing had to be precise, but as planned, the M.P. became distracted just long enough for me to leap up onto the fence, climb to the top as noiselessly as possible, then drop down to the sidewalk and freedom. My plan worked well, and I moved quickly up the street, only daring to look back briefly. I did not want to appear suspicious if the guard detected me moving away from the Navy yard.

My goal was to reach Times Square in Manhattan, but first, I had to find my way to the Brooklyn Bridge, which crosses over the East River. While walking, I turned a corner and faced the intimidating presence of a large group of young men moving toward me on the other side of the street. I had heard terrible stories about sailors found tied to lamp posts after being whipped to unconsciousness by the belts of local gang members who thought their girlfriends were, somehow unfairly, taken from them by the sailors.

I was very nervous as I walked across the street and directly to the group. I then boldly asked one of the guys for directions to the bridge. No problem; he was very involved in the group's conversation. He didn't want to miss a thing, so in very few words, he responded to my request then quickly moved away, catching up with his associates who had continued moving forward. The rapid beating of my heart slowly subsided as I took the direction he had given.

The only other time I crossed the bridge, I was aboard a bus going to the "Yard," so I hadn't paid close attention, not enough to notice the bridge structure's significant size, nor the distance down to the water far below. This time, very few people were on the walkway because of lateness, but I could see a man hunched over as he walked toward me. And, just as we were about to pass by each other, He mumbled, "Give me a cigarette!"

Indignantly, I responded, "Listen, bud, that's no way to ask for a cig.; try saying please!"

As he unfolded his body from his hunched position, he got taller and taller. He must have extended his height, rising-up six or seven inches taller than me. The smell of alcohol and sweat was excessive as he demanded in a much louder voice without changing the full sneering expression on his face, "Give me a cigarette!"

Images of terror raced across my mind during a struggle in which I imagined our fragile bodies falling about twenty-four stories to the East River. I fumbled with my half-full cigarette pack and handed him a cigarette. I then rapidly continued the mile and a half walk across the bridge, cautiously looking around to make sure no one was hiding in the shadows while planning a surprise attack. As I exited the bridge, my pace increased, and I deduced my direction to be toward Times Square.

My route brought me to the financial district known as Wall Street. My feelings of personal lack magnified in consideration of the significant financial transactions taking place there day after day. During the first few minutes, I imagined money in the form of coins passing like grains of sand into my hands, but my sanity soon returned, reminding me of the minimal amount of currency in my pocket.

Beyond each moment of my existence, thoughts and dreams had no future. Life had become an endless demand for immediacy. Fear and confusion established a significant deterrent to a means for survival. I had to find a way to make it through that first night, but I was apprehensive and scared of things unseen as I explored dark alleys and dimly lit streets. Then I realized fear would either consume me or spur me into action.

There was also a not-so-amusing irony about where I was. Sure, I was broke, but even so, there I was walking through Wall Street. In a few short hours, individuals would be rushing about, and business would be booming with massive amounts of money changing hands. I wondered, what would I be doing? How could I exist without the benefit of cash?

I finally reached Times Square, but after arriving, I had no idea what to do, so I strolled around to get my bearings while attempting to figure things out. A variety of delicious smells from restaurants permeated the air reminding me that my folding money and other belongings were still in my locker on the ship. So, with no obvious choice, I decided to trust my luck, be patient, and see what would happen. I was now dependent on a fate that had not been very gentle of late. It turned out to be a continuous struggle, especially during those early days, until I learned to find my way around. The school of hard knocks taught me that whatever happens to anybody is, with rare exceptions, entirely dependent on their past and present choices combining. The concept of my freedom was becoming more and more difficult to define within the existing circumstances.

Streams of people were crowding the sidewalks. They pushed and bumped, yet each person pretended indifference to the presence of every other one. In this city of more than seven million human beings, all acted remotely from each other. Yet, we were each a part of the masses where every person struggles to express some form of individual identity, then essentially surrendering to the widespread commonality.

Confusion almost swallowed me, but I slowly began to feel connected to this enormous herd. I realized the act of resistance I had taken now forced me to be alone as if thrust out from humanity. However, the simple fact of being human established contacts within the shared commonality from which few rarely escape, except through death.

My recent Navy experience and approval requirements were no different from being restricted, such as being in prison. Respond obediently without thought, deaden your mind to any question of having a choice. One must act like every other person in the group, or there will be hell to pay!

Freedom means having no restraints except through the acceptance or elimination of the particular obstacles or support that establishes each person's choices. We each experience freedom every time we make a choice. Yet, I had chosen to leave the Navy but still felt that I was not free. These taunting feelings would remain until I understood and accepted or rejected the conditions connected to my newly chosen existence.

While slowly walking along and observing the many different types of people, I became aware of two M.P.s intently inspecting the crowd from the street's outer perimeter. I believed they were searching for military personnel acting suspiciously, exhibiting drunkenness, or out of uniform. This incident drove me to avoid a possible confrontation by retreating to an area where contact with them would be less likely to occur. Because I was on the run, I needed to conceal my presence.

Sometimes I would approach a person and explain that I had inadvertently blown all my money and couldn't pay the subway fare to get back to the Navy base. After they paused for a moment while regarding me somewhat like an insect, only then might they hand me enough cash for the subway. It was sheer luck when I discovered a restaurant where I could buy a plate of spaghetti for the low price of twenty-five cents. The delicious smell of Italian spices was, in itself, almost worth the entire cost.

On the rare occasions of good fortune given to me by my latest benefactor, I would leave with funds enough to return the following day to eat again. I felt embarrassed at the necessity to beg. Still, my reticence slowly became overcome by the constant growling of my empty stomach. Two weeks later, I discovered that being clothed in a Navy uniform established a welcome to receive various benefits available at the U.S.O. My survival often depended on the food offered and which I readily accepted during visits to these facilities. It was never anything substantial, apples, oranges, candy, and other pocket food. They also provided towels and maintained a shower room where a person could bathe.

Though my existence was lacking in nutritional food, the U.S.O. never lacked in contributing educational benefits. They frequently provided tickets to museums, Carnegie Hall, Broadway plays, and even Radio City Music Hall featuring the Rockettes. Though my circumstances were far less than desirable, benefits bestowed by the U.S.O., while unknowing of my military situation, did make my rebellion far more tolerable. I was surprised to learn that the available tickets were often left unused, going out-of-date, and effectively wasted. I also found refuge in the Public Library, where I could read and stay warm during daylight hours when the weather turned cold.

I intended to reduce any chance of being apprehended, so I stayed out of sight the first night and each following night. I slept wherever I could find a place. Much of the time, sleep was erratic because I attempted to sleep standing up while hidden within concealment found in buildings' dark crevasses. I often awoke crouched in a sitting position with my head resting on top of my folded arms.

One evening, my confused experience of freedom took me a few miles beyond Times Square's bustle toward Harlem. On my way there, I passed by Saint Patrick's Cathedral and noticed that the front door was partly open. I accepted this as an invitation to enter. The experience of stepping out of the noise of traffic and directly into the sanctuary was profound. I became surrounded in peace after entering into the grand interior of the church. Sometimes, in moments of quiet such as this, a person faces life's reality. I found myself wondering, *Do I know who I am?*

It was a pleasant relief to be in that sanctuary as I sat on a wooden pew and meditated. The sweet scent of burning candles and lingering incense enhanced my experience of safety. I closed my eyes, and the blinding surges of emotional stress from the physical world slowly vanished. As if in a dream, quiet formlessness began to invade my consciousness. Colored flakes of fire ignited to form a creative foundation within this sanctuary.

There are no restrictions in the eternal moment, so my awareness began to expand. I could sense something strange living in this place of the mind; a vague image slowly materialized from nothingness. While I peered intimately into the darkly shaded movement ahead, the gray mass of an elephant gradually began to develop. Its vast body moved from side to side, and its trunk hung down like a giant arm in an extension of its large gray head. Deep brown eyes plead sadly for the privilege of existence. The grief of the world reflects from within those pools of brown as they seem to beg assistance. A large serpent-like chain encircled the elephant's tree trunk of a leg. I wondered how I might help a great beast like this? Then I heard words as if whispered in my ear, "There shall be no enslavement in this place of freedom!"

Freedom for the elephant then became a thing of the past, and his image slowly liquefies, melting like a dropped ice cream cone forgotten in the sun. Suddenly, as if in response to my realization of freedom, the chain burst. A flash of yellow transforms into a cluster of small ducklings surprised by the light of newfound freedom. They scurry about like ants exposed when the earth is upturned. The elephant's body completely transformed, becoming a living marsh where the yellow ducklings now leisurely paddle in an experience of total safety.

Rays from the sun are warm and filled with the lazy sound of flying insects circulating in colonies and uniting throughout the marsh. Cattails stand firm amidst deep green foliage: phallic symbols depicting evolving change. Life exists as a process of growth from within, changing into that which it has always been.

The smell of moisture combines with the heat of summer, validating the contrast of earthen elements. The base-drum sound of green frogs orchestrates the heartbeat of nature's melody; tones blend with the electric crackle of crickets. It is an eternal symphony forever declaring the alpha and omega of life.

A red-winged blackbird alights upon my shoulder. It cocks its head to one side as it nervously examines this strange new tree as if it is born of the marsh, not the reverse. When I blink my eyes, she flys off again, crying out a warning to all the other creatures of the swamp. It is a game she plays to give herself a vital air of importance. Sadness begins to fog my mind as I yearn for human companionship, yet I know all humanity is here with me in this suspended moment. The realization of truth is made manifest as the warmth of the sun begins to rise inside of me. The experience of unification is the uncompromised process of shared existence.

We are never really alone because humanity exists in the unity of one. There is no separation in this place. You are me, and I am you. He becomes one with her, and she gives birth again. It is the moment of ever-moving, yet never moving realization of life: the eternal now of all time and space.

We exist in this place as a symbol of truth without physical form. Frosty flakes of energy float lazily all around. Slowly each unites with another, and there remains one light; one truth, and one eternal now.

Together, we transform into the marsh's reeds swaying gently in unison with fluctuations of the warm summer breeze. Overhead a hawk in transcendental glide, wings fully spread, slowly circles down to fulfill basic needs.

The humidity becomes thick, and beads of perspiration form on the outer surface of awareness. A slight wave of heat precedes light summer rain, and the sharp smell of the marsh is pungent and delicious in a baptism of life.

Overhead a rainbow begins to form through transforming colors of pastel red, yellow, and blue. I can see only part of an unbroken circle. But I know the half-circle rainbow becomes complete within the earth. The colors change when touching the marsh, then swirl in dark ringlets integrating quietly within the musical symphony of life. The sounds, smells, and the sight of life can never be divided but will always remain a part of the eternal rainbow.

The blackbird calls out again to warn of my imminent return to this grand cathedral, where I now meditate. As this place of personal confession returns to my attention, I remember the reality of my moment in the sun and the point in time when flying as a blackbird loudly announcing to the world that we each must stay free.

Yes, soon, I must return, but I'll take a few minutes more to sit alone upon that yonder hill and feel the grass beneath my naked body. I shall contemplate the distant crested butte or soar high into the depth of the deep-blue sky. Most of all, I will always remember the wisdom of this life that is uniquely mine. I only need to take the time to close my eyes and see.

Now, I hear the ticking of a clock on some faraway classroom wall. It has no hands to point the time because there is no past, nor is there a future: we always reside in unity with the eternal now. The clock chimes the reality of this moment. In the school, a door swings open. A child runs excitedly onto the playground to join in the adventure of life with the other children. On the classroom wall, white chalk numbers appear on the blackboard surface: four, three, two, one, and I open my eyes; I must now return.

These moments of creative solitude were interrupted by urgings from my survival instincts warning me to depart this cathedral. I pushed aside my feelings and decided instead to spend a few minutes more, moving about the interior inspecting with respectful curiosity about the religious icons such as the Holy Mother caressing her child. This experience brought a sense of spiritual revelation into my fragmented life, a few moments of welcome, though temporary, serenity, and well being. Time passed quickly, and though I felt safe and desired to delay my exit, I also felt driven to resume coping with the challenges required for survival in the outside world. Departing from a holy sanctuary is a bit of a shock. I had returned to reality, as expressed through the noise of the city.

Moving on up the street, I soon found myself in Harlem. I had barely entered the business section when a man erupted through the door of a bar. He held both of his hands to the right side of his body as he loudly screamed into the silence surrounding him, "I'm bleeding! I only meant to kid that guy; why did he have to stab me?"

My mind went blank, and for what seemed an eternity, I stood as if frozen to the spot. My senses transformed, instantly becoming all of me. I could feel the smell of human blood penetrating my nasal passages; I instinctively spit the repellent taste into the gutter. That man's fear of death became my fear as I glanced around to see if anybody else was a witness. It was not a time to inquire about the nature of what this man considered "kidding." I was obsessed with losing my freedom. Paranoia and apprehension were constant companions, always pushing me toward safety, one way or another. I quickly turned and began following the path which brought me from Times Square.

The following day I learned that there had been a significant riot in Harlem a few months earlier pitting suppressed blacks and other minorities against white man's control. Black people had supposedly been given freedom many years in the past, but they experienced significantly fewer benefits while being shackled by poverty and prejudice. I felt somehow akin to the plight of these people who, taking action and in spontaneous acclamation, chose to rebel.

I made my way back toward Manhattan through a slightly different route and happened onto an abandoned subway about halfway to my destination. Heavy wire-mesh fencing had been stretched across the opening to prevent trespassing. However, vandals had torn the fencing apart, allowing entry for street people or anyone else desperate to risk the inherent dangers waiting within.

The day was passing quickly during my venture to Harlem. Now, as if pressed to fulfill an appointment, I wondered about the time. But time no longer carried any real meaning for me, so I returned my thoughts to the underground tunnel where street people were beginning to appear. They gathered in the hollow opening and were temporarily spared from social ex-communication: the punishment for existing as a blight on society. These people felt they had no freedom, yet they were free. They seemed to lack an understanding that the conditions where they found themselves were often self-imposed penalties reflecting past choices. The homeless have no societal constraints, but the acclimated realm in which they exist is just as constrained and conformist as everybody else.

These misguided beings were unknowingly sacrificing themselves to reflect the American government's position directed by certain powerful corporations that rule the business and political cultures. Unfortunately, many of our highest government leaders receive corporate money used in promoting their victory in elections. In this context, the citizens of this country thereby become nicely dressed servants for the rich.

This cave was a reminder of my recent visit to St. Patrick Cathedral. In retrospect, the church's quiet aura compared in my mind to the historical period (1715 to 1789), referred to as Reformation. From the smoldering discontent of enforced acceptance, inspired words had been spoken and written disobedient to the existing regime. It marked the beginning of a religious rebellion from which erupted the era of Enlightenment. With the emergence of rationalism came an end to the sacred monarchy, which blocked individual freedom to choose. The modern equivalent is the ruthless, power-driven corporate executives and their investors, who again exist as a monarchy. Their existence will also come to an end.

I watched through the obscured lens of my mind as the street people entered the cave and slowly transformed into dark shadows. These were not Plato's cave-shadows; they could never be confused as an illusion of something they were not, despite the horrible circumstances in which they now existed.

Thoughts of *Dante's Inferno* flashed through my mind. The seventh, eighth, and ninth circles: murder, violence, fraud, and betrayal. "Abandon all hope ye who enters here." Not only are many of these people the perpetrators of crimes against humanity, but often it's victims. This place is the personification of hell. It might easily compare to a dark pit, filled with unidentifiable living creatures gathered together for warmth and improbable protection from a danger which, ironically, enters with them in their expression of life. And when the winter months return, it will be like Dante's hell, the worst of seasons, with all the winter inhabitants condemned by the wind, ice, and freezing snow.

In retracing my memory, the end of that day seems opposite of every other evening dusk routinely hiding the sun and slowly casting life into darkness. During this time, people receive a brief reprieve from the revealing glare of daylight's truth. But there is to be no reprieve here, no apparent escape from the bleak existence in which these people find themselves bound. Indeed, it is not just the lack of resources that establish limits on each person's choices. Mental fatigue and hopelessness also contribute to their sense of lost freedom.

The "cave" is a place of faceless images carved out of the dark soul of the city where you find the same human outcasts who, for centuries, have represented the repressed and hidden sins found in every culture. It challenges the transparent mural of unquestioned magnificence claimed by churches, museums, concert halls, and sometimes exhibited on playhouse stages. Physical trappings only pretend to be the actual thing—the glory is each of us as highly capable and independent beings. The cave is as invalid a trapping as the churches—just the flip side.

The next moment, I fell into a sea of surging compassion, but these feelings quickly became drowned within a cry arising from deep within the caverns of my mind: the impression that there is no meaning anywhere. It was that sense of meaninglessness in which I had been thrust. It was Nietzsche's voice crying out from many years past when he declared in *The Gay Science*, "God is dead, but given the ways of men, there still may be caves for thousands of years in which his shadow will exist. And we—we still have to vanquish his shadow, too."

These thoughts ignited my fear, creating a mental alert warning me to depart this cave of denial where the significance of individual choice seemed lost. It was as if in the act of unholy semblance, a ragged page had been abruptly torn from the first edition of a Charles Dickens novel, then crumpled and dropped into the gutter without further ado. Such it was that fear seemed to demand of all humanity, "Leave this place immediately; you will find no justice here!" Perhaps the message is valid, but maybe justice and truth might somehow be found by the suppressed in such a place when viewed from an opposite perspective.

The whole scene seemed to highlight humanity's indifference to the unfortunate members whose very existence drags all human life back into ambiguous mental darkness and surrender. I want to turn my head as if this condition will, as a result, cease to exist. But the ultimate price of apathy is always higher than the cost of giving. When giving aid, the experience is of a mutual benefit; the contributor receives positive feelings through the offerings' act. These acts may also temporally free people from their greatest dread of all, the fear of death. However, without the fear of death, people would no longer have reason to look to the gods for immortality as projected to be in heaven and hell. Their gifts are mental projections, conscious or unconscious, bribing the gods for eventual acceptance into the otherworldly destinations. There are no worries about choice because everything is already perfect, except living life without thinking is no life at all.

A parallel to this exists when people of a weaker disposition fall back into mental and physical despair. In so doing, they carry with them a small part of humanity. Individuals seldom experience feelings of tugging or pulling from another person's fall; it is more subtle than that. Throughout the world, many unfortunate people who fall increase from one to thousands in a year. The effect can be seen and felt throughout all of humanity. Negative influences develop in the mind, and consequently, through this focus, the negativity manifests as bad experiences in one's life. Such is the process through which repetitive thoughts become actualized. And so it is in the opposite that positive thinking produces desirable things simply because one's mind becomes emotionally focused in a positive direction. In other words, if we focus on a condition, positive or negative, we are more likely to experience that same valuation.

Many unfortunates who are existing in the cave are victims of mental illness. During an extended period in the past, they received care in psychiatric hospitals. As time passed, the discovery and production of new drugs seemed to help control their dysfunctions. Most of the patients were released from supervision in hospitals and instructed to take their meds regularly. Unfortunately, regularity such as demanded is impossible to maintain while living under a viaduct or undesirable places. Consequently, medications are effectively rendered useless by the patient. This "medical treatment" becomes a placebo for the bean-counters and government officials who labor under the belief they are saving society by eliminating mental hospitals and their monetary cost.

I was abruptly roused during the depths of these observations when I heard a man's voice quietly say, "It's rather unusual, isn't it, like a ghost town within the bowels of the city?"

Startled, I quickly turned to see who spoke. At first, it was as if I were listening to the echoes of thoughts created within my mind. Perhaps I had allowed myself to become too deeply engrossed in the cave because standing next to me was a thin man dressed in nondescript wrinkled clothes. He had a scraggly beard, and his hair was in the process of transforming from the dark brown color it had once been to become a movement of white expressing the revolution of life which occurs naturally among most middle-aged people.

I tried to respond to his question as a matter-of-factly as it had been asked, "Yes, you're right; it's like a living nightmare!"

The truth is, in my apprehension at the sudden appearance of this man, I wanted to move quickly down the street, but I learned long ago that if faced with a dangerous animal, one should never bolt because to do so establishes you as prey. I don't wish to imply that this fellow was nasty, except within the realm of possibilities, but I had not yet taken the time to reject such a dubious conclusion.

His response to me was quick and adamant, "You do not want to go into that place! You very likely would never come out alive!"

Thanking him for his concern, I said, "Frankly, I had already come to the same conclusion myself."

I grew warmer during our meeting, and we talked for a few minutes more, at which time I revealed my circumstances. My new acquaintance questioned me a little further, "Have you found a place to sleep tonight?"

I hesitantly answered, "No, I'm still searching. Most of last night, I tried to sleep standing up while leaning against a building," I continued emphatically, "and it was not a preferred lodging!" We both chuckled at my indignant pretense of anger expressed through the transparent understatement.

He told me to come with him, and he would show me where I might stay. It was not without reluctance that I followed him, and when we passed by a city trash can, he grabbed some discarded newspapers which seemed to be reaching out as if in anticipation of our arrival. It was not much further to a nearby park. With a wave of his hand, a steel bench under a tree would transform into my bed.

He smiled as he announced, "This will be your bed for the night." He then handed me the newspapers, "These are your blankets; they will keep you warmer than you might imagine. Just spread some of them on the bench, lie down, and place the remainder on yourself. Don't linger here too long in the morning because the police patrolling this park is not at all sympathetic to vagrants. However, I'm sure you won't feel so comfortable on this bench that you might push a snooze alarm and oversleep."

I nervously laughed while thanking him for the newspaper strategy he had taught me. I turned to look once more at my bed for the night, but before I turned back around, my new friend had quietly disappeared into the darkness. I puzzled as to where his sleeping place would be that night, and I asked myself, why had he been kind enough to help me?

I sat thinking for a while about the day's events but soon felt it must be getting quite late because the street traffic noise had begun to slow and become quiet. I felt exhausted, so I prepared my "bed" as instructed, lay down, and fell quickly to sleep. I did not sleep deeply and was aware of noises during the night. At one point, I awoke to emotional voices in the distance which, I surmised, was a man and a woman arguing in a parked car. Then I listened to a drunken man talking angrily to himself about not being respected in his workplace by fellow workers who had blatantly accused him of being a drunk.

Later, I thought I heard a muffled sound that seemed close by and threatening to me. I sat up quickly, instantly awake, and carefully studied the bushes in the outer surrounding area, but I could see nothing which might present a source of danger. However, I continued to feel as if someone was observing me, and I rationalized that it might be my new acquaintance, the stranger, maybe checking on my safety or just looking to see if I was still there. Even now, reliving that moment creates goosebumps running up and down my spine. I do not believe it was the stranger. However, I think that being awakened by that inner instinct was a gift handed down through my family lineage, arriving age to age from ancient ancestors whose alertness was required to escape the dangers of prehistoric animals. It may have saved my life that night, but I never discovered what seemed so ominous and imminently threatening.

It was not one of my better nights of sleep, and without question, I had not forgotten my preference for a regular bed composed of a mattress, blankets, and a pillow. However, a newspaper bed under a sweet-smelling maple tree in the park was far better than trying to sleep with the smell of cement while leaning against a building's cold exterior. I felt fortunate to have a place to lay my head, even if it lasted only for one or two nights.

The following day I thought I spotted the stranger walking down the street not too far from the park. When I started to call out to him, I realized we had never exchanged names. And, because of the early morning noise of traffic, he would not hear me yell. He seemed to have a definite purpose as he disappeared into a crowd of people. I wondered if I would ever see him again.

The stranger had acted as a valued friend, yet I didn't have the presence of mind to acknowledge his act of human compassion in my apprehension and fear. Neither did I ask his name nor adequately express thanks to him. I have consoled myself with the realization that he, too, hadn't felt vital importance in knowing my identity. His participation in our meeting seemed to suggest that the act of helping a fellow human was more important than such things as exchanging names. I concluded that he was just a good Samaritan living on the streets of New York City. He was the first person I had the good fortune to meet without having to qualify or justify in some way for having the gall to exist as an outsider, perhaps because he too was an outsider.

There are those in the mainstream who may lack empathy for the situation in which objectors such as I floundered and individually expressed objection through spontaneous or willful rebellion. In the beginning, I rationalized while viewing myself as a rebel that my actions were in opposition to the war in general. Previously, whenever I thought about any fighting going on in some faraway place, it had seemed unimportant. It had now become a big issue in my life. I realized that combat is where the seriousness of human death and destruction is supposedly modified when blithely referred to as "police action." For example, in such places as Korea, accounting for all the deaths combined, there were 1.2 million human beings, men, women, and children who died due to the so-called "police action." Compare this to a large city like Denver, all the living inhabitants just disappearing from the planet, never to be seen again. You could be visiting with a person one day; then, in what seemed like minutes, they disappeared, gone forever, their potential lives unfinished. Many small children and adults might be found dead in the street, their bodies rotting, and food for the rodents.

The individual members of a country's military usually have no idea of the real reason they are fighting. Indoctrination has been by nebulous words pretending symbolic justification, words like freedom, flag, justice, or even God. (What arrogance humans have when we act as if an omnipotent being needs anyone to fight for it.) The words do not describe the government's actual motivation, and become especially suspicious if used when big business interests control the government.

I was confident that my objection was just and to the benefit of most people, except, I hoped, not for the profiteers and wealthy beneficiaries of war. Most people don't think to ask how certain members our country, such as often found in the nuclear, coal, and oil industries, are wrecking the world's environments. The consequences of businesses that turn away from responsibility while expressing social and environmental indifference provoke hate from other nations worldwide. Because they have nothing better to do, smaller countries don't just decide one day to hate Americans. They feel that they are opposing significant injustices inflicted by a big bully called the U.S.A. Ironically, the American public rarely questions the justification rhetoric of our government directed by big business.

Like most other young men in the early stage of life, I had expressed very little interest in politics, nor did I understand or have a fear of death. Instead, I felt confused, anxious, and angry at having my freedom taken away by the military in the government's name. A battle raged in my head about what I should do. I had felt no anger toward anybody, especially people living in far-off countries, where I had previously never given much thought.

The government initiated a mandatory draft that denied young men their right to choose whether they wanted to participate in the military or not, effectively taking away their right of choice. The same government demanded giving up one's life for the same freedom they have taken away. To this day, it makes no sense!

According to the government's laws in the United States, a person must have a religious affiliation to justify their conscientious objection. Whatever their motivation, many people have no such association, so they sometimes conclude that the only way to take a stand against war is by non-participation. Incidentally, the definition of the words conscientious objector is a person who, based on religion or principle, refuses to bear arms or serve in the military.

It is a well-documented fact that fifty percent of people in religious affiliations are moving away from organized religion. At the same time, many of these same people declare individual spirituality. This departure from mainstream religions will even further reduce the number of government-sanctioned religious conscientious objectors.

While A.W.O.L., I returned to my bench in the park many times to feel some semblance of freedom and safety. It became a place away from home. I could not return until after I accepted my confinement destiny during an unknown period in a military prison.

It did not take too many months to realize that living on the streets was an undesirable quality of life. I had survived by selling my blood, posing for a group of artists, and various other means, which required no personal identification. I finally wrote a letter to my parents asking them to send a few of my civilian clothes to a recent acquaintance's apartment where I could retrieve them. With the proper apparel, I planned to get a job and, even temporarily, start living a better life. I knew my parents would be worried, even though I wrote and tried to reassure them that I loved them and was doing all right.

I received some of my clothes about a week later, but three men were waiting with handguns pointed at me when I went to retrieve the clothing. These fellows turned out to be with the F.B.I. It was a frightening experience, looking into the barrel of a gun, then handcuffed as if posing a significant threat to national security. However, I was somewhat relieved to be apprehended and returned to the military.

The following six months were hellish: confined and isolated in a cell-block at a local brig. I did not know why I was selected to be placed in such radical confinement away from the general prison population. This cell-block area intended to admonish particularly rough treatment to approximately fifteen men awaiting the same type of court marshal that all the other prisoners were to receive. In response to the brutal conditions, two men attempted suicide by breaking a window and slashing their wrists with the broken glass. One prisoner banged his head against the cell-block wall every night for extended periods. There was never a response by the guards to subdue him. Another man, having attempted suicide, was given a diet of diminished rations, which consisted of a spoonful of potatoes, one small bite of meat, and so forth. He once told me that it was worse than being given piss and punk, usually known as bread and water. I would sneak food into his cell whenever possible.

Each cell measured a 7-foot length by 4-foot width and included a thick wire covering about 7-foot high through which guards dumped a bucket of cold water on any prisoner falling asleep. A rag within the bucket then rattled into the cell, followed by harsh words commanding the prisoner to clean up the mess. There were no books allowed, and no mattress, only two blankets, one to lay on, and one with which to cover up while sleeping at night. Every cell was very much like a grave.

The days seemed to drag on with neither meaning nor end. Mail, if ever received, was censored or destroyed. After my release, I learned my mother had written informing me that Dad was close to death after his appendix ruptured. The guards had discarded the message.

During my time of confinement, I used the thick wire cell-covering to exercise and increase muscle mass. I intended to intimidate the guards who frequently came into the cells badgering and insulting individual prisoners. Two of these marine guards, one small, the other a big man, entered my space. The little man did most of the insulting and agitating, while the larger man seemed to accept his position as a bodyguard for the other. I did not talk or respond in any way except to stare at them, which appeared to be effective because they finally stopped bothering me after the first month. I dreamed of looking them up after being released from military prison, but it was the last thing I wanted to do when finally released.

There was also a sadistic sergeant who wore a metal cap on the sole of one of his shoes. When he came around, we were called to attention and told to stand nose-toes to our unit's door. He would then slowly saunter, click-click-click to the block's back area where his movements stopped. Deathly quiet broke like dropped glass with the sound of a cell door opening. A guard commanded an unfortunate prisoner to double time to the perimeter of the block. When the prisoner turned around the back corner of the cell block, the waiting Sargent hit him in the gut. The man cried out and whimpered in fear. No one ever knew what rule the prisoner had broken. During that time, I decided that if ever chosen to run the gambit, I would not go down without a fight, even if it meant spending more time incarcerated. Luckily, I didn't get selected.

One day I was told I had a visitor. My older brother was in New York, investigating the possibility of living there. I was delighted to see someone from home because it had been several months of virtually no verbal communication. Having remained silent for so long, I found it challenging to talk with him. Feelings of emptiness and sadness filled me when I learned he returned home after a few days. His visit with me was only that one time, but it meant a lot to me.

After several months, the time for my trial finally arrived. At the tribunal, they gave me the option to go back to duty or continue my confinement in a military prison; I opted for the latter. The "lawyer," who was appointed to represent me, answered very boldly when asked if the number provided was my serial number. He responded, "We so stipulate!" That was the extent to which the Navy offered legal representation. Nor did I have the opportunity before the hearing to consult with a real defense lawyer. After months of waiting in a military prison, there had been no interest in my reason after having committed such an atrocity as being away-without-leave.

Eventually, after returning home, I asked my parents how the officials had come to find out about my whereabouts. I was sure my mother lied when she said my letter must have inadvertently dropped where the Federal Bureau of Investigation (F.B.I.) spotted it when they came to the house looking for me. Her story seemed utterly bogus; however, I am sure that the mere presence of F.B.I. agents can be highly intimidating.

Whatever their reason, I felt disappointed and betrayed that my parents had presumed to take my choice from me. They may have thought it would be best to conform to the wishes of the government. Or they may have acted as many parents do under similar circumstances; that is, in the pretense of love, they conform to the herd mentality or status quo in making and justifying their decision. Perhaps because of this same kind of brainwashing, I had betrayed myself by allowing my activation into the military service. I chose the same manner by which all the other young men my age entered the service—the blind leading the blind.

I survived my time in confinement and was eventually released to return to civilian life. I did not then, nor have I ever regretted my rebellion. I have striven to live my truth, as reflected in this writing. I once had the opportunity to have my negative military records revoked. I refused this option as a show of principle in what I had attempted to do in standing opposed to the outrageous injustices perpetrated by our big business controlled government on peoples of other countries and citizens of the U.S.

Surviving in the streets of New York without money is not a pleasant task. And choosing a life of individuality and authenticity can also present problems, but far less over time than experienced by people who give up their true selves in the name of acceptance. The path I walk now and continue to walk in the future is my choice and responsibility. Each person's way is his right, and as Robert Frost wrote in his oft-quoted poem about two paths crossing in the woods, "I choose the one less traveled by, and that has made all the difference." *The Road Not Taken, The Poetry of Robert Frost*, Published by Holt Rinehart Winston 1967.

I hope never to forget the painful lessons I have learned through bitter experiences in the unhallowed dimensions of human existence. Haunting memories and the sounds of suffering echo from many a dark cave: these are the places where brave battles of life and death will always exist.

Perhaps some resistance to war will continue, if only by the few. The positive fraction, which stands in opposition, helps quiet the noise that erupts during continuous wartimes. Such are the times when great masses of human beings can at least hope to live through their entire lives. Rebellion demands that freedom must gain acknowledgment as a natural endowment to all of humanity. When that time appears in humankind's history, we shall each be free to choose our unique path of life. I wonder, will society ever be ready? Freedom is choice, and with our present choice comes responsibility for the consequences of our actions.

# The Job

Every year during my youth, come summer vacation, our mother would sternly direct my brother and me to "Go out and find a job and don't come home until you have one!" The idea she conveyed was to walk down the street, enter every store, and ask the owner or manager if they needed help. She said this was a far more productive and profitable strategy than just sitting at home, wishing we had some money. And, she added, "God knows I don't have any money to give to you."

In response to her argument's logic, combined with feeling a slight bit of intimidation, we went job hunting. We walked separately, wondering which of us had the best side of the street. We both experienced feelings of apprehension, but we always came home with a new job. I never asked how much the job would pay. It didn't matter to me because if the person in charge told me I could start the next morning promptly at 8 a.m., that was all I needed to hear.

During our youth working various jobs, our resume (as if either of us had such a document) would have been like an employment kaleidoscope revealing a colorful variety of different roles. We eventually became adjusted to Mom's plan, frequently researching possible work beforehand by talking to friends or staying alert to "help wanted" signs in store windows.

Our varied employment history included jobs like digging worms for a bait shop. The worst thing about that job was when sleeping at night following a day in the field, I tossed and turned, attempting to escape in dreams about worms seemingly out to get me. We also set pins at a bowling alley because the automatic pin-setting machine didn't yet exist. One of our (err) colleagues here was a man who acquired tobacco from cigarette butts found in the gutter. After removing the paper covering, he smoked the brown weed in his pipe. The smell was like something borrowed from an outhouse, so we would get even by relieving ourselves, urinating on the hot steam pipes. We soon declared him the winner because the combined smell became unbearable. We also delivered telegrams for Western Union, had paper routes, mowed lawns, busboys, locker room boys at the swimming pool, sold *Saturday Evening Post* door to door, and worked as a hospital orderly. Upon reaching the mature age of 16, I became a lifeguard at a city park lake for three summers. This wide variety of positions during my childhood influenced and directed me to move in an entrepreneurial direction during my adult life.

But this is jumping too far ahead in our employment history because we learned a valuable lesson from the experience of our very first job, which we worked and shared as a team. The exposure to which I refer happened when I was five, and my brother was the ripe old age of seven. However, unlike many of the following years of summer work, we were still too young to need to be intimidated by Mom's command to "Find a job!"

Our first job was not a summer job, and that winter, the city experienced a significant snowstorm. Coincidentally, on the same night of the storm, we overheard our mother and father talking about not having enough money to buy food. At that moment, we were not hungry, so I don't think the reality of not having enough food to eat penetrated our awareness. We took it for granted that dinner would be on the table. It always had been there, and because it was there, we never went without eating. But on that particular night, we became motivated by the sadness and worry expressed in our parent's conversation.

Before going to sleep, my brother and I talked briefly and decided we could earn money to buy food by cleaning neighborhood sidewalks blanketed with snow.

The following day we found two shovels in the shed behind the house and set out to fulfill our goal to earn money. We intended to help Mom and Dad escape from the struggles people have whenever trying to elude the pain of poverty. Maybe I should mention that we didn't have the mindset to work an eight-hour day, and indeed not a forty-hour week. We just wanted to earn enough money to buy some food so that Dad and Mom wouldn't feel unhappy.

We started the following morning by walking down the street, knocking on doors, and asking whoever answered the door if we could clean the snow from their sidewalk. We had pre-established a standard charge of ten or fifteen cents depending on the particular walkway; we hoped our price wasn't too outrageous. As it turned out, our plan succeeded better than expected. We experienced what we considered a vast amount of financial success. Later that day, when my brother held our accumulated coins in his hand, it seemed to me that he was displaying a fabulous treasure equal to that of Monte Cristo.

As the day wore on, it was progressively getting colder and colder, so we decided to clean one last sidewalk before calling it a day. We chose a house on the block, which, of course, was a corner residence. We wanted that place because the sidewalk was much longer, and by cleaning it, our customers would think us justified in charging more money. We decided twenty-five cents would be acceptable.

A frail, gray-haired lady wearing a white bathrobe answered our knock on the door. When reflecting on this early stage in our lives, any person over twenty-five would have seemed old to us. The lady agreed to our business proposal then quickly closed the door because, as she said, she didn't want to let all the heat out of her house.

As we started cleaning the snow off her walk, we had the added motivation of doing a particularly good job because, after all, we were charging the lady twenty-five cents. It took longer than we had anticipated because the snow began to freeze, but with the job complete, we rapped on the door to get paid. No answer! We knocked again with the same results. We persisted, but the lady wouldn't respond to our summons.

We wondered, "Does this woman think we are working for nothing?" We were angry because, of course, we felt cheated. We talked about shoveling the snow back on the walk but couldn't bring ourselves to mess-up the work we had completed so well. Our efforts would become meaningless. But as we walked away, feeling sad and angry, we threw a couple of shovels full of snow back on the sidewalk, then partially cleaned it up again. This action made us even more unhappy because in our eyes it was equal to throwing a glob of paint on a Rembrandt painting, if you will excuse the comparison.

Our negative feelings began to ease as we approached what was to be our final stop, the grocery store. Before entering the establishment, we talked (that is, I listened to my brother talk) about conducting a question and answer session with the grocer. We wanted to make sure that we were not spending beyond our means. After the inquisition, endured by a pleasant grocer, we purchased a loaf of bread, some lunch meat, a head of lettuce, and two small pieces of penny candy, which we considered an appropriate reward for our work. We ate the candy while quickly returning home with our gourmet acquisitions.

Upon entering the house, we proudly made our presentation to Mom, who appeared shocked after inspecting the paper sack's contents. We had not informed her of our look-a-like Sherlock Holmes eavesdropping event the previous night, so she seemed unaware that we had overheard the conversation between our father and her. She hugged us and told us what good sons we were. It became evident at dinner time that they had solved their financial problem earlier that day because we ate roast beef and potatoes while my mom bragged to my dad about what good boys they had the extraordinary fortune to be blessed. (I may be embellishing her words slightly.)

We were proud of ourselves and never told our parents about our experience of not being paid at the last house because we felt it was somehow due to our inexperience. Even today, I sometimes think that we are each responsible for the world's weaknesses and problems.

In the meantime, we tried to understand why the lady hadn't paid us. Maybe the woman was sick, taking a bath, or just hiding because she didn't have the money to pay two small boys who she considered far more able than she to do the work. Perhaps she also thought we owed it to her, kind of like a tax collected by the government.

A few days later, when riding my tricycle in the neighborhood, my attention was drawn by a group of people standing around whispering by the corner house. I noticed a big black car with heavy maroon-colored curtains covering two side windows of the vehicle. I approached some young boys who were standing nearby and asked them what was happening. They told me their second-grade teacher who lived in that house had died after suffering a terrible illness. They continued by saying she was a wonderful lady who was just about every kid's favorite teacher. It passed through my mind that had she lived, and she might have been my teacher when I reached second grade.

Later that day, I told my brother that the same lady had died who lived at the corner house. He instantly knew I was talking about the lady who we felt had cheated us. There was no need to say much more about the incident because he would be in second grade, and he already heard that a new teacher at school would be teaching his class. We never discussed the possibility that the old teacher may have died while we cleaned the snow from her sidewalk. I had feelings of sadness for that sweet second-grade teacher, and I also felt a little guilty because, in our anger, we had labeled her a mean person. Maybe she thought we were among the many kids who might be or had been in her class. There is a lesson to be learned in everything. Could it be that her last act of teaching was her gift to us? If this is so, we learned not to make judgments about people before understanding the contributing circumstances.

# The Internship

DURING ZACH'S YOUTH, he dreamed of becoming a medical doctor. When looking back, he wondered what had inspired him to choose such a vocation. A significant influence was his friend Russel, whose father was a doctor. As an M.D., he enjoyed a lofty status among his patients and other people who knew him. Russel's family lived in a large house and enjoyed many other desirable benefits, such as membership in a country club where Zach sometimes was invited to go swimming with his friend Russel.

Zach's dad was a salesman in the appliance department at a mercantile store. Zach could remember the day his father came home happy and told his wife, "I got the job and will start next Monday!" No one had any idea that he would spend the next thirty-five years of his working life at that department store.

So, when Zach decided to be a doctor, he essentially concluded it was merely a matter of going down to the hospital one day and applying for the job. Any thoughts in obtaining academic qualifications did not enter his mind. What he did observe in his dad's success in securing his new position was a willingness to work.

Zach had no desire to excel in schoolwork, and consequently, the appropriate reward for his lack of effort reflected rather bland grades, neither sparkling nor too bleak. However, to his credit, he took summer jobs in hospitals intending to familiarize himself with the business of medicine.

He worked as an orderly in many sectors of the hospital, including the mental health ward. One particular night he was feeling happy with the last night of the late shift because his revolving schedule changed to a morning shift the following day.

That evening while working in the psych ward, they received a new patient who was very menacing and entirely out of control. Zack, lacking significant stature, felt even smaller when appointed by the nurse to direct the patient (who seemed to grow more massive and substantial with the progression of Zach's assignment) into a private room reserved for patients in a high state of anxiety, such as this patient exhibited.

The patient did not seem at all intimidated when Zach, standing as tall his approximately five-foot structure could stretch, slowly approached the raging patient. The man continued to yell and act belligerently. Then, reaching over Zach, he grabbed a sizable metal-and-leather chair (the weight of which Zach surmised, must have quickly surpassed Zach's body weight). He then picked it up by its front leg (which Zach visualized as being only slightly smaller than his leg) and pressed it high over his head while staring threateningly at Zach.

In contemplating the situation, Zach's actions, which followed, may have been a little less heroic than he later cared to admit: he searched the area for a safe place to which he might retreat. But from the corner of his eye, he caught the color of something blue moving in his direction.

Bless the nurse; she had called for aid from a hospital police officer to help in securing the patient (should Zach by remote chance need any help). The patient quickly became calm as he became aware of the officer's presence. Or it might have been, as Zach told his friend later, that he became aware of Zach's bulging biceps. The man quickly went into the previously designated room and became silent.

The policeman began expressing an interest in the nurse now that the patient had became subdued, so Zach concluded the emergency had ended. A short time later, his shift was complete, and, with a deep sigh, he went immediately home because of his reassignment to the early shift the next day.

The following morning as Zach approached the hospital, feelings of apprehension followed him as he entered the psych ward and could hear the door-lock click loudly behind him. The nurse instructed him to engage the patients and try to get them involved in reading magazines, doing puzzles, or anything else that might constitute engagement. The primary area in the ward was a large room with benches, chairs, and tables placed around the central section.

Many patients were already occupying the benches and chairs, while others were still entering the area after breakfast. Zach became involved in his job, offering reading material to patients. He was surprised when faced with a patient who had been declared dangerous and placed in the ward earlier that week. Zach weakly smiled as he offered him a newspaper. Before the man could respond, Zach realized the man was looking beyond him, gazing at the new patient who had arrived the previous night. The new patient now entered the area and was standing directly behind Zach. Zach turned around to face that fellow, and at the same time, he realized he had turned his back on the other patient, so he continued turning around to face the other patient.

The room became hushed, and Zach glanced around to see what was happening. The patients throughout the ward were staring at him. In his confusion, he had been turning around like a toy top slowly spinning between the two men.

Later it occurred to Zach that the patients must have concluded that his assignment to the ward must have seemed appropriate. It did not surprise him when looking back that they seemed to accept him after that day as one of their own. Zach enjoyed his new position of trust and acceptance by them. However, he sometimes wondered, was it the patients who changed in their approval of him, or was it, in reality, he who somehow changed?

"In an insane society, the sane man must appear insane." (Source unknown)

# To Sleep

*To die, to sleep-*
*To sleep, perchance to dream- ay, there's the rub,*
*For in this sleep of death, what dreams may come...*
—William Shakespeare, *Hamlet*

IT HAS BEEN A STRESSFUL DAY at work, and returning home, I feel tired and sapped of strength. After warming up a dinner comprised of three-day-old leftovers, my fork disinterestedly picks at the food. Finally, I push the food aside and retire to bed much earlier than usual. An escape into the cover of night seems like the most liberating thing to do. Sleep can be a creative place, a state of mind where hopes and dreams sometimes appear, offering promises of a new reality.

Perhaps today's failures and frustrations will become exposed by examination and unconscious revelations through what is often called the mind's dark side. The dark side sometimes seems harmful and unhealthy, existing as an unearthing of things that can cause a child to cry out in fear at night. That child had been me, and now as an adult, I am sometimes visited and deeply unnerved when anxiety returns to invade my dreams. I have read that the subconscious is composed of repressed memories and experiences seeking escape. It can also be the home of hell, a frightful place where each person's devil resides.

While waiting for sleep, I hope pleasant reveries will satisfy my desire for a new reality in life, even if only existing on loan for tonight. As my body slowly relaxes, my pillow transforms into a woman's soft hands, gently caressing my head. My eyes close, then quickly open again as my mother's stern image thrust forth from within my memory as if to shock me back into her reality. I resist by turning over in bed while squeezing my eyes shut once again.

While listening to night-sounds which project illusions of faraway places, the loud demands of an angry motorcycle protests through the sounds of thunder, its owner's disenchantment with the so-called "normal" life, the life of the herd.

I despise being part of the pack, but I don't know how to escape. Acceptance by the herd requires living up to a potential established through repetitious conditioning assigned early in life. Society demands one's compliance with existing rules. It is a universal agreement requiring a mask to be worn presenting a persona of sameness. These hoods are instrumental in establishing the status quo in society.

I have known for some time that it is a form of death to live a life that is not the truth of one's self. An authentic, self-actualizing person expresses an innate quality, described as a kind of genius that varies in every human being. If not acknowledged through use, it may lie dormant for years and even seem dead, but through commitment and dedication, a person can resurrect the grand gift of authenticity.

How can people not fear death if they resolutely sit back, allowing themselves to die slowly, then buried in the mass grave of sameness in which each person is responsible for digging? I know this is the same tomb of fear I consider myself of having created. I live with this curse of anxiety because I pretend to be like everyone else, to do otherwise is to risk possible ex-communication from humanity. I am anxious because I am afraid of change, especially from life to death.

Making believe to be that which I am not, I offer excuses by pretending to be a victim of my childhood. And during the years of school, especially at the university, I, like many of the other students, believe that the demands of academia is to live "correctly." These expectations repeat the same social standards, the established rules of thought and communication each student brings with them from their home. These rules flow from an uncut umbilical cord, a conduit supplied by the family's conformist social behavior. Rebellion during the teens creates a momentary promise that the new generation shall reject the false beliefs generated by society. Alas, the establishment, those old impostors of truth, quickly extinguish the fires of the young.

Some schools require students to dress like soldiers in uniform, marching without a true individual identity, always to the beat of the same drum. Repeat after me, again and again: Never question authority! You must give your life to the discretion of the "authorities" in charge! These people are substitutes for the human gods, Mom and Dad.

Competition and mass production require everything done inside the boundaries of a box. However, outstanding instructors, even though sometimes fearing retribution, encourage students, "Look outside the box; bend the rules and use your wonderful imagination to produce something new!"

Companies in the business world, corporations like J. C. Penney, Sears, Montgomery Ward, K-Mart, and others are disappearing from the earth because they refused to acknowledge changes occurring in society. Companies rush to hire recent college graduates to bring new ideas for change. But these ideas are quickly rejected by the same company leaders who claim to have a desire to keep up with the market through innovation and change. These leaders soon perceive a possible loss of power and prestige by things done differently than in the past. "We must not risk! Keep things the same; no need to change; these are the practices through which we have achieved our immediate success, our glory." Were not these the same words Jews and others cried out when the Nazis were becoming more assertive and nasty in Germany? This is in no way meant to downplay the monstrosities of Nazi regime,

But what is the answer to my life? I need my job to make a living. I receive fair monetary compensation, but I feel empty and without meaning, existing like a robot following a life of automation. I live as if caught in a nightmare from which there is no escape.

A line from Shakespeare's *Hamlet* crosses my mind: "For in this sleep of death, what dreams may come—." Even in dreams, I repeat behavior carried over from my waking state, then chastise myself for things gone wrong. My guilt originates from my fear of standing against the values of the herd. I have feelings of having sinned, (sin in archery—missed the mark) though I have done nothing wrong. I am single and without familial responsibility. No one relies on me, nor do I rely on anyone else. I fear death because I do not want to leave this world without discovering my actual purpose for being here.

If I don't take care of myself, who will? Unfortunately, many people think they will receive an affirmation of worth by pretending to know what is best for any other person with whom they come into contact. However, I am the only person who knows what my life lacks and what I must do to find the courage to arise from this state of inertia, this state of death.

I compare my situation to that portrayed by Albert Camus story of *Sisyphus* who is condemned by the gods to push a boulder up the side of a mountain only to have that rock roll back down repeatedly for all eternity. To live like this would undoubtedly be a meaningless life directing thoughts toward suicide.

But in another rendition of this myth, Sisyphus fools the gods by giving himself entirely to the task he is facing, and in so doing, creates self-definition and meaning within the assigned task. He commits himself to study all aspects of the boulder and every other nuance of the immediate environment in detail. Sisyphus's problem doesn't just go away, it transforms incoherence into meaning, and his life became an expression of fulfillment and creativity. He defeats the gods of retribution. Through commitment, he finds purpose. I must confine myself to live by this same principle.

I hear the distant warning call of a train communicating to me the possibility of living somewhere else: existence in a place with a beautiful job where the only demand is that a person uses their innate skills and potentialities. That is the place where I will find new adventures and meaning.

The transition from the state of waking to that of dreaming is like magic. A dream finally invades my mind. It takes over without the benefit of conscious choice, unfolding like a train coming out of a tunnel. I can't stop this train of my own doing. As if a god, I choose from moment to moment creation's development. Doing otherwise is a betrayal of self and all of humanity. I know dreams are the creation of the dreamer who, through illusions, symbolically acknowledges personal ownership of the demands posed by his vision.

The dream transforms life into a place where wild animals move like a mist through the forest, across a meadow, and down to a flowing stream. They follow instincts of purpose to fulfill the driving needs of life. They are drawn by thirst, and like all the other animals, they need water.

Carnivores also bring their demands to this place of flowing water, and if successful as hunters, they will eat to the fulfillment of their hunger and preservation. All the lower animal species express an instinct of continuity through the act of living within each moment of their lives. In contrast, human beings often sink to various levels of nihilism. To cease trying is to cease living, no matter what age a human might have reached. Life after the age of fifty-five is just as important as the years which come before. It is not a time in one's life to simply sit back doing little more than await the arrival of death.

The path of humanity leads toward a secondary, often undefined goal or purpose. Survival can usually be obtained quickly without significant risk. But man consciously knows he is choosing and in most environments has for the object of his choosing many different forms of sustenance. A person may want to read a book when driven by the purpose of mental fulfillment confirmed through the test of life experiences.

This path may contain hidden dangers, too. Predators of different types can appear as if having been conditioned by their mental makeup to disrupt the hero's intended journey. A human predator of this kind may take the shape of a smiling face concealing the desire to dominate or control others because of a lack of self-control and meaning in their own lives. They seek self-confirmation, but their method is never effective because they focus on the perceived deficiencies of other people, not on their own.

I feel entirely comfortable with this life within my dream. But as I descend deep within my vision, I am surprised by the sudden emergence of tumultuous happenings coming from a mural reflecting the appearance of living existence. It projects images from within the stone wall of an ancient Aztec ruin, a manifestation of circular movements turning in upon itself.

A mist now pervades the area; deep white clouds foam around two frightening shadow figures engaging in a wild dance: a celebration of life and death. I stand transfixed in the outlying shadows, afraid of being seen by these dreadful beings.

My thoughts turn to my mother as the angry face of an animal composed of smoke suddenly appears then quickly disappears. I want to hide, but in the past, I have experienced memories of things I thought may have happened in real life, but was that only existence seeming like a dream?

Now I can see petroglyphs drawn on the adjacent stone wall, but closer scrutiny reveals the markings as graffiti, alerting to the presence of dangerous gangs in the area. I feel fear starting to build up within my mind, but I realize I am here as a witness. A sacrifice must be fulfilled, but I do not know the player's identities, nor even a hint of the victim's life or reason for the possible execution.

I am dazed by what I think is the effects of a drug somehow slipped to me; perhaps it is peyote. I remembered an accounting of the Penitente Indians, who believed that peyote reveals the future.

But, I have received no warnings predicting the future. I only feel confused and wonder how I could have become drugged. Had a hallucinate been sprinkled onto the leftovers I ate for dinner? Did leftovers signify that the truth of life had no more meaning than profound repetitious consumption unto death?

I awake abruptly, feeling smothered by the pillow from which I had received comfort earlier. At this same moment, I can feel a fresh breeze pass over me, and I realize what the sacrifice demands. I feel as if I have somehow learned the way to redemption and an escape from conflicts of self-estrangement.

Three months later—

It has been a stressful day at work, and upon returning home, I feel tired and sapped of strength...

# Notes from the Dead

Dave slowly pushed the gurney through a tunnel passageway in the basement of the hospital. It had rained most of the day, and the ground outside became saturated. The rainwater followed the path of least resistance, and as is its tenacious nature, had begun leaking through the seams of the ceiling and walls into the tunnel. Dave remembered how Carlsbad Caverns were carved out by water flow in the same process during prehistoric times. The tunnel's leaking rainwater had shorted the lights out, and areas of darkness concealed sections of his route to the morgue. He struggled to distract himself from the fear lurking inside his mind.

Dave was fourteen years old, out of school during summer vacation, and had luckily landed this job in the city during the summer as a "floating orderly" in the city hospital. He felt fortunate because it was a short walk from home and did not require the cost of city transportation. His initial employment was an assignment in the emergency room. The medical staff was usually too busy to pay attention to anything other than their work. But the primary function of his new job involved moving bodies of deceased patients from various wards in the hospital to the morgue. One of the supervising nurses alerted him whenever the need arose. She was also creative in finding other things Dave might do when not busy fulfilling his primary role.

You might assume that a fourteen-year-old kid would experience a significant amount of fear in handling dead human bodies, but not so much in this case. Dave's primary concern originated from the possibility of doing something wrong and the consequence of losing his new job. Of course, he needed the work, but not just for the money earned; he also had dreams to become a doctor, eventually. This present position should provide an appropriate environment and opportunity to learn about medicine.

Earlier in the day, Dave had received a brief training from an experienced orderly named Pierce. For the most part, he showed Dave some of the problems experienced while doing this job, so it was not Dave's first experience in the tunnel. However, not anticipated during the orientation was the dire effects of rain.

His first day had started, and the person whose body Dave was now moving to the morgue had died of a sickness that included internal bleeding. The deceased had been a tall man measuring over six foot four inches, so when Dave attempted to move him from the hospital bed, the man's feet became hooked on the bottom end of the bed-rail. His feet were hidden by a sheet which extended outside the bed-rail. The pressure created from pulling at the body, caused an outflow of blood through the dead man's nose and mouth. It was messy, but Dave quickly wiped the blood away with a towel before anyone could see what had happened. He was afraid this display of blood and death might somehow be due to his clumsiness and lack of experience. He managed to leverage the sheet-covered body onto the gurney, then move it to the elevator, which responded to the touch of a button by descending to the basement with its cargo.

When Dave entered the concrete basement passageway, the smell of wet concrete and humidity combined to make it more like a tunnel or a cave. While he pushed the gurney, he became acutely aware of the wheels' clicking sound each time they bumped over a crack in the concrete floor. The cart would jump a little each time it happened, and the dead body would respond with a slight bounce. He continued to push as carefully as he could, but just as he reached a dark point in the tunnel where the lights had shorted out, the gurney hit a more significant bump, causing the corpse's arm to drop and begin to swing back and forth. The fingers almost touched the floor. Dave later admitted to experiencing some apprehension from a vision of the dead returning to life, but unfortunately for the deceased, it was not to be. He carefully lifted the arm (as if he might disturb the dead man) and placed it back on the conveyance. He then continued at a slightly more rapid pace on his trip to the morgue.

The tunnel runs south to north for approximately one hundred fifty yards from the elevator entrance and then turns to the west. Dave had just about reached the turn when he began to sense the unmistakable acrid smell of formaldehyde drifting down from the morgue.

At the end of the west tunnel was another elevator of much older vintage than the first. It opened from both sides, one side for entering or exiting to the basement, and the other one served the morgue. After ascending to the street level, the moving elevator's mechanical grinding sound slowed and stopped with a loud echoing clang. He opened the noisy door and stood looking into the darkness of the morgue, waiting for his eyes to adjust, but it was too dark. All he could see was a small amount of light through the French doors on the opposite wall, which seemed like a football field away. He later found that the glass windows revealed an outside courtyard with a small amount of dull light reflecting off the rain, which gathered on the asphalt.

Dave began to recall the brief training in which he had learned that he could locate the light switch just outside the elevator, but now when pushed, it didn't respond. He remembered Pierce telling him that you must return to the same wall-switch turning off the light to return it to the on position. So, Dave began to move carefully toward the dim light at the opposite side of the room where the lights must have been turned off, maybe after an ambulance delivery. However, as he moved across the room, his hand, which he was waving out in front of him like a blind person's cane, kept brushing against "objects" covered with sheets. Dave felt inspired to move more quickly but didn't dare risk knocking over one of the other gurneys. There is no need to explain further how in the darkness that night, Dave experienced an unwelcome discloser of bodies. This experience would occur again and again in the morgue during that summer.

He finally reached the opposite side of the room and switched on the lights. Upon closer inspection of the area, it became evident that ambulance drivers or orderlies from earlier shifts had pushed their body-cargo into the morgue and fled as quickly as possible to avoid possible retribution for not doing a complete job. It must have been a busy time at the hospital because previous attendants did not place any of the seven bodies into refrigeration. Dave began to inspect the individual refrigerated sections extending from floor to ceiling in units of four, which were each designed for one body per frame. Though somewhat perturbed, he could understand the lack of diligence by the earlier shifts in not completing their job because all of the lower sections were full. The problem was the smaller bodies deposited in lower units (by an uninformed or lazy person) left only the upper for heaver cadavers. The solution demanded Dave move the smaller of the deceased into the top sections; then, he could place the more cumbersome bodies in the lower levels.

As Dave began working to move the smaller bodies to the top levels, he quickly discovered that the lighter the body, the higher up he needed to place it to preserve space. This process was awkward and required patience and time. At one point, he found a cardboard box in the upper left-hand corner of the refrigerated unit. Upon examination, it revealed a baby's burned body remains, perhaps found after being dumped into an ash pit. There was no way to know what had happened, only the absence of life, a condition shared by all the other bodies, large, small, young or old, male or female.

Moving what seemed like a massive group of bodies turned out to be much less stressful than he had anticipated. After opening the door to a lower refrigerated unit and pulling out a lengthy rectangular tray, it was just a matter of positioning the gurney with the foot end lined up, then lifting the cart while holding the sheet and allowing the body to slide down onto the tray. He then moved the smaller bodies up, one at a time. After working at this task for several hours and having finished, he pushed all the empty gurneys down the tunnel to be conveniently found and returned to use.

He had worked long past the time for his lunch break, but he had lost his appetite, so he only purchased a chocolate donut and a soft drink in the cafeteria and sat down at a table to contemplate his experience. He felt pleased but somewhat dazed by his return to humanity. While eating the donut, he suddenly became aware that he had not washed his hands. He quickly put the donut down on the table and glanced around to make sure another person hadn't realized what he had done. He wondered what, if anything, he had learned from this experience about medicine and life and death. He continued his job as an orderly, doing the same work during the whole summer and asking himself the same question, but he could never seem to find an answer.

One day a friend asked him what it was like working with the dead. He told Dave that he thought his response would address the issues many other people have about death. Dave already concluded that the question refers directly to the person inquiring and their real concern, which must be, "What will happen to me after I'm dead?" He sometimes responded by saying, "What do you mean, what happens when you die? Nothing happens; you are just not here any longer. That is the whole point of death; life has come to an end. If you haven't found your life's purpose by that time and have not done what you came here to do, and you definitely won't be concerned."

# The Swarm

Allen's exit from the city bus is a block or two sooner than initially planned. Now free and breathing deeply of the fresh air, he finds relief from feelings of smothered incarceration. It is not unusual for him to react this way when using city transportation, but conditions are much different today.

Suddenly, his brief freedom is distracted by a loud sound, a high pitched noise like a human scream projected into his consciousness by the mechanical-breaks of the same city vehicle from with he had departed. The surprising sound startles a significant number of swallows roosting in a nearby tree. In response to their momentary panic, the entire flock has exploded into the air; they converge, swerve, and soar in rapid flight. It is an exhibition of group fear in which they instinctively fly together madly creating an undirected crescendo of sound as if they have been transformed into one giant being.

At first, it is as if Allen is encased within the sound, and he begins to feel at one with the flock. Then the illusion expands, and he imagines that the large group of birds has somehow entered his body and is currently flying around in abandon in the area of his stomach. But the birds are not any happier than he with this turn of events, and they seem desperate while frantically seeking escape from this newfound, yet undefined, place of confinement.

Allen pauses by the same tree which was abandoned by the swallows. Then, with his eyes closed, his mind conjures up a swimming pool laid out in front of him. Long thick strands of rope, kept afloat by stripped buoys, lay on top of the shimmering turquoise water. Allen is aware that these are dividing lines intended to establish select areas in the swimming pool to keep swimmers separated when competing in the water.

In his mind, he can feel his toes curling over the edge of a raised platform placed at the end of the pool. Then, bending at the waist, he drops his arms in a vertical position, puts his fingers next to his feet, and then poses with knees bent. He has become a large gauge spring wound tight and straining to release. Suddenly, the illusion disappears when Allen is startled by a loud bang: the cracking sound of a car tire passing over a manhole cover in the street.

The sound brings him back to reality, and when looking up, he sees rows of houses lining both sides of the road. His mind momentarily flashes back to the strands of rope dividing the pool into lanes just as the dwellings seem to have done to city streets.

A man hurrying in the opposite direction passes him, and Allen smells the smoke from a cigarette which has been quickly inhaled, then exhaled, polluting the warm fall air. He wrinkles his nose in repulsion and holds his breath while moving away from the smoke. A crackling noise coming from under his feet is the sound of dead elm leaves which have been rejected by the tree's community clusters that decorate branches of the ever expanding trees. Allen doesn't understand why, but he has a feeling of empathy for the discarded leaves. Thoughts of graduation cross his mind.

After walking a couple of blocks, at the corner of the cross-street in front of him, a college building looms darkly in his mind like a foreboding castle concealing a dark, green monster. Allen slows the pace of his step as he moves closer and closer to his destiny.

Other swimmers are also arriving a bit early, and are already entering the school. Some of the boys utilize backpacks to carry their gear, but another group tightly clutch small, colorful duffel bags, just like the one which seems to have become permanently attached to Allen's gripping hand.

The churning in his stomach increases as he walks through the massive doors into the hallway of the school. The end of life, the Omega, is loudly declared by the school's entrance slamming shut behind him. The sound summons the memory of his recent experience in the chamber of a mausoleum where his uncle's dead body was interned. When the crypt door was dramatically slammed shut, the sound thundered in finality throughout the halls of the building. At the slamming of the door, his uncle became a fading memory, a reminder to Allen to treasure every moment of his life by following his own dream. He whispers to himself, "I must win my event!"

Two of his teammates catch up with him; they walk together, talking and laughing. They are obviously nervous and seek security in comradeship, pretending that nothing important is happening.

Swimming is a sport with limited or no dependence on teammates. In almost every event, swimmers exist alone; their competition is found in the timing of their previous swim. The real game is actually located within their own mind.

The boys become quiet as they descend the stairs to the locker room. Their attention has been captured by the smell of chlorinated water used to disinfect the pool. They begin to sweat as a result of the thick, pungent air which increases in density when combined with steam from showers which are being taken by other anxious swimmers.

Allen's swallows seem to have grown into chicken hawks seeking escape from his stomach. They begin to burst into flight, then calm down as he finally discovers an empty locker and changes into his swimming suit.

The area has become very crowded as more swimmers arrive with dreams of achieving the honor of "All-State" in their respective individual and relay team competitions. However, each swimmer is aware of his own level of excellence, and he knows what chance he actually has in the contest. Each contestant is mindful of his likelihood of winning, and for most of them, winning is only a dream.

The time passes quickly to the beginning of Allen's heat. A thought from his physics class enters his mind, "Can an infinite universe exist as a turquoise swimming pool when experienced as I, in my mind, do now?" He reminds himself that it was he who chose this moment in the world, including this stressful feeling of agony which carries with it the beautiful possibility of being number one in the state: the best swimmer in his event.

As if from a far away hillside, Allen hears an echoing announcement being made above the sounds of excitement generated by the crowd. All the swimmers in his competitive heat are beckoned to report to the starting point at the end of the pool.

Responding quickly, he automatically begins his pre-race routine by entering the water, taking a few warm-up strokes, then exiting again. He breaths deeply to fill his body with energy. He shakes his arms, then circularly moves them intending to loosen his muscles. He also hopes to distract his mind from the sensation of the flock of birds presently flying within his stomach, but the birds have multiplied into angry throngs and are now attempting to escape through his mind.

As he drops his towel behind the raised platform, his mind enters into eternity. A voice on the public address speaker demands, "Swimmers, take your mark!" Allen steps forward, his toes curl around the edge of the racer's platform at the end of the pool. As he leans into the crouching position of his racing dive, he can see the bright reflections on the water divided into lanes by thick strands of rope.

All is as deathly quiet as a church chapel on Monday mornings until, over the speaker system, a male voice commands, "Swimmers, take your mark!" Then a slight pause and, "BANG," one shot from the starter's gun, and the silence is broken.

Friends and family scream in excitement as the swimmers propel their bodies through the air toward the water. At that same moment, Allen's birds, unseen by the crowd, vanish into the nothingness from which they have come. They are chased away by the excited screams of people vicariously sharing in the hope and anticipation of a gifted human being who has spent hour upon hour practicing for this event. This race will last less than sixty seconds, but miles of laps have been completed in commitment to a dream which is about to become a reality.

Upon the last stroke, when the winner touches the swimming pool wall, the difference is often only one or two one-hundredths of a second separating first from second place in a sprint. Imagine, practicing by repetitiously swimming the length of a pool so many times that at one point, you must quickly get out of the water before you vomit and spoil the water for the practice of others. Then the coach says, we will now do racing dives and turns for the next hour or so, then call it a day. Don't forget to keep your grades up or you will be disqualified from the team.

Through all this work, Allen has honed his skill to the point of instinct as sometimes observed in the flight of birds. Committed people always know what I am writing about. Allen paid the price toward winning the race, and now has the honor of having achieved All-State in his event. He isn't any richer in the financial sense, but there is a good chance he will win a scholarship to a university.

I have a special pride in this accomplishment because the winning swimmer I write about was also the author of this story using my father's name, Allen, as a pseudonym.

Sadly, I must announce that after graduating from school, I was activated in the service. While in the Navy, and swimming in a Ninth Naval District aquatics competition, I managed to win two first-place trophies. It is a privilege to have competed with all the other swimmers, including some who had been in the Olympics. Each was endowed with the pride and drive to reach within themselves to something they considered to be of higher value.

# Paved in Brick

Summers, when my brother Bob and I were just little guys, our mom and dad would send us to visit our grandma in Trinidad, Colorado, a small town in the southern part of the state. We would pretend dramatic suffering and "death by travel," used as a pretense to avoid change from our everyday existence—not unlike most of humanity's resistance to change. However, we experienced a quick recovery from the excitement and anticipation of our upcoming adventure.

The very next day, we boarded the train carrying us to Grandma's house. Our father talked briefly with the conductor, who said he would keep an eye on us. Upon overhearing their conversation, we felt as if treated like children, so we instantly became resigned to keep an eye on the conductor. Like all men of the world, we thought we could handle anything, and of course, it wasn't as if we hadn't completed this same trip the previous year.

The journey would take about five hours, including layovers in Colorado Springs and Pueblo. To prevent our starvation, Mom had sacked a couple of peanut butter sandwiches, some potato chips, and two small bottles of milk.

During the first hour of the trip, we sat attentively and gave ourselves to the train's experience. We could smell smoke blowing back to us from the coal-burning engine, and we listened to the harsh clacking of steel wheels beating repetitiously like the sound of a flat tire once heard on our father's car.

Bob recalled when we put a 1939 penny on the rail so the passing train would flatten the coin. We had immediately discontinued this activity after a friend told us it would cause the train to crash. We stood aghast as he claimed it had happened several times before in other parts of this town of about 7,000 residents. We visualized the terrible prospect of our small coin, causing a horrible train wreck with thousands of people dying, all for a 1939 penny's flattening. We would probably be apprehended, dragged by huge chains, put into a dungeon, remain forever, and finally, not smell very good as our bodies rotted away. We couldn't imagine what either of us would look like as grown men, so it seemed necessary to project through imagination our young faces aged by the growth of long gray beards.

While the train was moving down the track, we held temptation at bay for what we thought was an unbearable amount of time before we finally dipped into our lunch sacks. Some people might find eating lunch two hours before the designated noon hour a bit too soon. But, in our minds, paper containers, such as sacks, made loud distracting noises and also could be extraordinarily cumbersome if a person happened to get pressed into action during a train robbery.

We adjusted quickly to our new-found freedom; the benefit of liberty was fast becoming the norm in our lives. However, we knew our independence would end when our grandmother sent us back home in time for the fall semester. I could never believe that she became firmly convinced that all children (such as me) would choose to leave their summer vacation and return to school. I also couldn't believe that she welcomed the solitude of winter as a time to reminisce after spending the summer with her grandsons. The truth is, she didn't have time for reflection of any kind; besides, she only saw us on a part-time basis. She was always too busy to be overly concerned about where we were or what we were doing during our visit in such a small town. Her gift to us of total freedom was balanced only by our need for food and subject to a strict schedule at the house: breakfast at seven, lunch at noon, dinner at six o'clock. The program was mandatory, no exceptions, except when grandma declared it otherwise, and she was almost always liberal with us.

Bob and I usually followed dinner with two or more hours playing in the house's massive basement where grandma stored past remnants. Cloth rags could be found and tied around our heads, whereby a transformation occurred, changing into pirates cruising the ocean searching for loot. Or, with a quick twist of imagination, we were fighting alongside Zorro. Then, as exhaustion reached a threshold, we went to our room and were soon dreaming peacefully of slaying dragons and such. By nine o'clock each night, the whole house had slipped into a quiet sleep.

Grandma's house, now a museum called the Bloom Mansion, was also where she made a living by doing what she called "boarding roomers." I now think this was a preview of nursing homes as we know them today. However, most of her pensioners seemed to be a little more self-reliant. Perhaps this skill was necessarily required to survive the Great Depression, which was still dragging on in the nineteen forties. Grandma never had enough money or food to spare, but whenever a hungry tramp came begging, her rules made it mandatory that he complete some small task assigned as a condition of his meal.

I didn't think of myself as a snob, but I rarely associated with older people at the house, and they didn't seem to harbor hopes of playing with me either. That was all right with me because I was almost sure they didn't have the nerve to ride on the back of my red tricycle while I burned laps around the porch.

It was during this same age, about five or six years old, and I was outside playing on the porch when my ongoing fantasy rapture was interrupted by a commotion inside the house. During a moment of misfortune, a bird flew inside one of the rooms, followed by the voice of a frightened woman who loudly proclaimed, "Death is coming to this house!" And so it was a few days later, the same prophetic woman died in that room.

Grandma's boarders all seemed ancient in a distant kind of way, so the incident made a minimal conscious impression on me. Though in retrospect, it was my first crossing between superstition and death. I could conceive only of life, especially in the vast experience of my imagination, where the awareness of death was just a word used to describe an unknown part of life. The end of life rarely has a place in the existence of most children, whether happy or sad, passionate involvement lives in whatever they may be doing or thinking.

On the south end of Trinidad stands a mountain called Simson's Rest; to the north is Fisher's Peak, which is just about a mile away. Bob and I enjoyed hiking and exploring whenever we had the opportunity, most of the time. These two mountains existed as a challenge for us. Simson's Rest hovered over us like an angry school teacher using intimidation as a teaching tool. Fisher's Peak beckoned to us with the mystery of its Peak pointing up at the sky. We were confident it was an active volcano with lava and stuff like that. (At this point in the story, it is probably unnecessary to remind you of the incredible imagination endowed to almost every child, especially if they are not discouraged in using it.)

As the summer passed, we grew bolder and more adventuresome. Simpson's Rest ascends from the outskirts of town through a pasture where, as we made our way, we came upon what we considered a vast herd of ten aggressive beasts ready to stampede and trample us into the ground. Neither Bob nor I could tell the difference between a cow or a bull. However, not one had horns, but oh, they looked big as elephants and bold as hungry lions inviting two young humans to lunch. Yes, they were especially monstrous when viewed through the minds of small boys just trying to make their way across the pasture. We considered ourselves fortunate when finding a fence through which we managed to escape with our lives. After all, we were not on a safari hunt. We wanted these animals to know that we intended them no harm; we were only trying to make our way in life. We felt that we were quick and crafty after maneuvering to safety with our bodies intact. That is to say; we ran as fast as our legs would move us. The beasts must have been put in shock by our speed because they increased their rate of savagely devouring the grass.

I have no memory of ever climbing very high on this mountain. There were just too many things to see and do around the lower area, sparsely occupied by a few farmhouses and two or three abandoned shacks.

As we walked, we met other kids about our age who, after a brief conversation and no formally announced fraternity, joined with us as if they had also been on the same exploratory venture. They told us a story about having met an unusual man the previous day. It seems this person, so they said, could make milk come out of his body. They were on their way to see this feat again, and the man could usually be found in a shack just up ahead. They invited us to join them in observing his trick. One of the neighborhood boys, Matt, already knew of this man. He said that the people from around the district of his home called the man Cyclops because he only had one eye.

We exclaimed, "Hey, sure, lead on!" (Where was Zorro when we needed him?) Sure enough, after we walked a short distance more, there, by an old shack, stood a man with one eye and a peculiar half-smile on his face. Earlier, we learned he lost his sight during a beating from which he barely survived in the past.

He spoke with a voice full of delight, "Are you all here to see me do my trick?" Several of the other kids who had been there the day before said, "Yeah!" And that was all that was required for the man to turn and walk into the shack. A couple of our fraternity members followed him, but Bob and I went to a broken window in the shed where we could observe from a slight distance; the man was already unbuttoning his pants.

No one had ever anticipated the need to tell us about people like this, but almost instinctively, we knew this was not a show our parents would appreciate. The man did his thing, then asked if we would all like to see him do it again. We felt somehow disillusioned because we had watched the man do something we had no understanding or any real interest in observing. And, having viewed from outside the shack, we felt no need to decline the man's invitation to a second showing. Bob and I walked away, joined by two of the other boys.

On our discovery trip, we began to adjust to our natural capabilities and strength. We grew more confident through our confrontation with wild cattle-beasts and our visit to Sicily's mythical island, where we met a Cyclops and lived to tell the story. My brother and I never mentioned the Cyclops experience again until revealing the secret in this writing. We only hiked a short distance farther, then we bid the other boys, "see ya," and we returned home. We heard a rumor the following year that the Cyclops had met his death. He died with clay dirt stuffed in his mouth, possibly done by the same men who had knocked out his eye the year before.

A few days later that week, we were ready to continue our adventures into the outlands, so we set off early one morning to conquer Fisher's Peak. This mountain is north of town, so consequently, our route was through town. At one corner, about halfway across the city, three boys were standing as if waiting for us. When we got abreast of them, one of them challenged, "This is our part of town! Do you want to fight?" Bob did not pause for a second, turning toward them, and stepping forward, he responded, "Yeah!" One of the boys said, "We were only kidding." They turned and hurried down the street.

I was proud of my big brother even though we were almost always in conflict: we hit and shoved, yelled, and using a minimal cuss word vocabulary, we sometimes cussed. There were times when I hated him, but this time, he was my hero—at least during the following hour or so. We stopped at a drinking fountain at the next corner, and though we weren't thirsty, we drank some of the water then squirted it out through our pursued lips. I think it was somehow a way of leaving our scent. Lions in the jungle do that too, you know.

As we neared the outskirts of town, we came to a low flowing river. There was a bridge crossing about a half-mile down the way, but we thought it essential to investigate the waters for marine life: things like octopus, whales, sharks, and other such fish which may have ventured inland from the ocean fifteen hundred miles away.

We took off our shoes and socks, then rolled up our pants to keep from getting wet as we walked into the deep, about six inches or less. We posed with hunched backs, our hands reaching out, ready to grapple with all the water monsters not too frightened to respond to our challenge. The water was cold, but it felt good after our barefoot dance on the hot sand. We lingered for several minutes investigating the water, but we didn't even spot a minnow. So, after putting our socks and shoes back on, we pushed forward toward Fisher's Peak. It was now only about a mile away, and it seemed to be growing bigger and higher each step we took.

We finally reached an area of growth at the foot of the mountain. From out of the weeds issued life sounds, which we concluded must certainly be rattlesnakes. "Watch this!' cried my brother as he hiked up his pant legs and ran, high stepping through the foliage. I quickly followed his lead and never questioned for a minute that this might not be the best way to pass by snakes without getting bitten. We knew his maneuver was a success upon reaching the far side because we were both still alive. The warning sounds may have been the back-leg sound issuing from grasshoppers communicating eros, but one can never be sure of such things. Our lives never lacked bravery, err—hardly ever.

We could see a wide crevice daring all climbers to reach the first tier of the mountain high above. We looked upward as we rested a few minutes in the shade. If we were to achieve success, the challenge required us to move over a path that someone or something had somehow created on the dirt side of the cliff. To say the trail was narrow may be an understatement because even with our small frames, to succeed, we had to press against the dirt wall, which gradually rose about twenty feet above the rocks below.

I waited as Bob went first. It took him some time to reach the other side, where he announced that it was easy, "nothing to it." Neither did it look easy, nor did I find it so, and I froze less than halfway across. I felt terrified to move even one inch more, either backward or forward. After some encouraging words from Bob, such as, "If you don't hurry, I will leave you here all night by yourself!" I wanted to cry, but that would make mud out of the dirt on my face, so I inched forward despite my fear and a small amount of earth decorating my face.

Then, while looking at the position of the sun, now in the west, Bob yelled to me, "Stop, we are running out of time, and we will have to come back over the trail again to get down." He then started returning on the path toward me. His return required me to move in the opposite direction from which I had been coming. There wasn't room to turn my head without throwing my weight out of balance, so I started the return route without looking forward. I imagined a future in which my battered and bleeding body lay stretched across the rocks below.

At my funeral, Grandma would be mad at Bob because he is eighteen months older and should have known better. All the people would say things like, "Too bad for Jim; he was a good boy!"

My distraction into imaginary thoughts about death and glory brought a pleasant surprise. During my time in vivid imagination, I had returned to the starting point of the dirt path. I had made it back, but Bob was now having a hard time moving across the trail. I rooted him on because I didn't want him to get hurt. "If you don't hurry, I'm going to leave you here all night by yourself!"

We were quiet on the way home but decided to return following the route we had taken when crossing the river. We arrived and waited a moment to get down the sloped embankment before quickly taking off our shoes. While looking back at Fisher's Peak, we each related how we had practically climbed to the top, and without any fear, risked our lives.

We couldn't have been paying close attention to the immediate area because a gang of Mexican boys had surrounded us as if out of nowhere. Their leader wanted to know what white boys were doing in their river. We told them that no one told us it was their river, and we were crossing over on our way home.

After a brief conference, their leaders decided that a fight would determine our destiny. I would be fighting one of the guys in their group so they could see who would win. It was evident that their fellow wasn't any happier than I with the results of the conference. But with a great deal of cheering for him and none for me (Bob wisely kept his mouth shut), we came to grips. At this point, I tripped my opponent, but in that same moment of the fight, I held him steady, preventing him from falling. Almost instantly, he knew who was the strongest, but I had no interest in fighting another, but a bigger kid in their gang, so I made no further effort to upend my rival. The group soon became bored with the hugging and grunting, so they separated us.

Bob was off to the side when I caught his eye. Without speaking, we started running toward the bank on the other side of the river. They yelled and ran after us, but they had little motivation and knew we had too much a head start, so they stopped their pursuit. On the way home, I speculated that they undoubtedly had stayed back because they feared the great fighter, me. I would turn and say, "We want to fight you, one and all. Just come forward and meet the Lone Ranger and Tonto!" Anybody watching could see two superheroes laughing and bumping shoulders together while moving down the street.

We arrived home that night just in time for dinner. We never took food or water on our adventure trips, nor did Grandma ever ask why we always returned so ravenous.

Two of Grandma's clients were blind: one man, Raymond, was a bit strange. He sometimes paid my brother a minimal amount to guide him on walks downtown to the railroad station. Upon arriving at the station, Raymond held his hands to his mouth with no train in sight and projected a loud yelping noise attempting to mimic a train whistle. Perhaps this was his visualization of traveling with the other passengers toward faraway places. TOOT, TOOT, TOOOT, they were on their way, but Bob stood there with Raymond on the brick-paved street. And, of course, he felt embarrassed by the people who were laughing at such a spectacle. We never knew how Raymond lost his sight, but railroad memories seemed to remain quite vivid in his mind as a high point in his life.

The other man, Mr. Thomas, during a sad time in his life, had attempted suicide. He held a gun to his temple, then pulled the trigger, shooting out both of his eyes. His failed attempt at death seemed to appease him because he didn't try again. When I first heard this story, it didn't occur to me that he must have had a reason to want to die. I could only wonder how anybody could do such a thing to themselves. I felt my body shiver when thinking about the shocking reality of what he had done. After I grew older, I guessed that he suffered from depression, losing a loved one, or losing money due to the recession.

Mr. Thomas kept a jar of hard candy in his room, which he sometimes shared, one piece each, with Bob and me. Then came an unforgettable day when Bob and I could find nothing to do. A vision of Mr. Thomas' jar of candy crept into our minds. He had not offered us candy for several weeks, and the thought of sweetness brought salivation. We wondered how we could get into his bedroom where he stashed the candy? We decided our answer was in becoming second-story men by climbing up the rose trellis to the porch roof.

We did not pause, and when we reached the roof and were standing outside his window, we could see it was partially open. Climbing through the opening into his room, we quickly spotted the jar of candy on his dresser. Quietly, we began slowly moving forward... At that moment, the door opened, and there stood Mr. Thomas. We froze, hardly willing to take a breath. He demanded, "Who's in here?" We did not reply and, as fast as we could, climbed out the window and down to the yard. We were sure he knew we were the trespassers and would surely tell our grandmother. Once again, we would end up in prison, spending the remainder of our lives after a beating with a cat-o-nine-tails. Mr. Thomas did not tell a soul, but we suffered for weeks from guilt and regret.

My grandmother boarded pensioners for as long as I could remember, then she too finally became one of the recipients of the same service herself at a different house. A few years later, she had dementia, and our parents eventually had her moved to the Pueblo State Hospital for the mentally ill.

One summer, our family visited her, and we found her with other patients in a big patio area enclosed by wire screening. There seemed to be no supervision except that a large black woman, also a patient, who, with a fly swatter, was moving among the patients, swatting them while loudly reprimanding them. It was apparent that she hadn't received proper treatment from white people for many past years. Our family caused a great commotion while pleading for her to stop. Our noise caught the attention of an orderly who grabbed the flyswatter and told the lady to sit. Things settled down after that.

The orderly took my dad and mom at their request to a private room to visit with Grandma. My brothers and I quietly remained outside and waited. We sat by a fountain where an angel's sculptured hand reached out as if blessing all the patients, staff, and visitors at the hospital. Somehow it didn't seem as if Grandma had ever received her fair share of the grace.

Even when I was still little and visiting her at the Bloom Mansion, I couldn't understand why Grandma had been outwardly prejudicial against black people. There were but a few of those folks quietly living in Trinidad. I don't know which part of town they lived in, but I occasionally saw them shopping downtown.

The next time I attended a funeral, it was my grandma's. During that time, a thought crossed my mind concerning brick pavers, used like bricks to pave most of Trinidad's streets. Morticians brought Grandma's body to a cemetery grave and then sealed it in the same clay from which the pavers get produced. She always wanted to be buried in a mausoleum where the worms couldn't get her. Perhaps she got a place in nature's mausoleum, indirectly fulfilling her wish.

What I experienced at her funeral has been repeated several times since, often seeming so much like a play acted by a cast of confused survivors. The women cry dramatically, but only after the opening of the privacy curtain, exposing the area where they sit separately from friends in the chapel. This melodrama repeats at the graveside. I feel compassion for people in grief, and I am confused about when and how they might best express their sorrow. Funerals might act as a celebration of a life lived, a reminder for the living to live the duration of their own lives fully and with passion. Funerals are for the living, not the dead.

In their discomfort with being at a funeral, people often say strange things afterward, such as, "Didn't she look nice?" I always chuckled to myself to think anyone dead looked particularly "nice." We never know where the person has gone, but indeed, they are not present any longer except within the survivors' memories. If the deceased, in any form, somehow would attend the proceedings, it might happen with them expressing the same amused irony.

My mother and I visited a nursing home a few years ago. We went there to see my aunt, diagnosed with terminal cancer. When we entered the building, my aging mother said, "Don't you dare ever put me in one of these places!" I responded with deliberate fake-compassion as I replied, "Mom, you must start behaving yourself." She glanced at me with a twinkle in her eye and a mischievous smile accompanied by a friendly elbow thrust sharply into my ribcage.

The first thing we observed was a lot of old folks sitting in wheelchairs. It was my perception of "old folks" because that was how they were acting. However, we could see that many were not without curiosity because when we started moving through the corridor toward my aunt's room, they looked us over like we were part of a parade they had been waiting for hours to see. I whispered to my mother that I hoped they thought we were clowns bringing happiness to this place. She responded with another elbow to my torso.

Looking into the patients' faces, I saw remorse, defiance, and indifference, but there were also some friendly smiles. I wondered if some of those smiling faces might harbor hope that these strangers had come to visit with them. Maybe it was my imagination, but they all seemed to be waiting patiently for something unstated, though perhaps merely passing the time with a singular air of inevitability.

Later, while my mother and I talked with my aunt, I again became aware of the same sense of certainty, an awakened awareness of one's mortality. As Aunt Louise spoke, sharing some of her experiences in life, she mostly expressed in the past tense with occasional reference to the environment in which she now found herself. She then whispered, as if in unacknowledged acceptance of her pending death, "No one ever knows what tomorrow will bring."

I remembered that she and my uncle had traveled worldwide for the last twenty years of their lives. Many times when they returned home, it was only to book accommodations for their next trip. All travelers know of the projections into the future required in anticipation and preparation for this adventure. Perhaps my aunt was in her way, even at that moment, planning for some great trip with which she would surprise us later. My uncle has been dead for two years, so she must travel alone this time to a final unknown destination.

As I listened to her, she seemed happy and child-like, smiling more than I remembered her ever doing so in the past. She had been a teacher, even wrote one of the first books on special education.

My mind then turned to the memory of two young brothers visiting their grandmother for the summer. They had a vague awareness of "going home," and they too were caught in an experience of the inevitable. I could hear the echo of their voices crying out, "You are dead; I killed you!" "No, I'm not, I killed you first!" They run around playing Zorro, crossing swords with the sound of cannons, and the thrill of memories from some movie they believe they will never forget.

When one boy falls, feigning death, he immediately resurrects and is alive again. He is no longer a fallen hero, but active and quite ready to sacrifice himself repeatedly for the cause of glory or any value perceived as a declaration of doing or being right. He may even choose to accept being viewed as a villain, although he is somehow always waging his fight for human rights.

Perceptions of immortality live through the hopes and beliefs of many men and women. For others, death is not the enemy, but merely the first condition of all life in which nature paves the laws of existence in brick.

When we wished my aunt a final farewell that afternoon, Mom said she felt like it would be nice if we could get a cold beer. Mom was never very friendly with my aunt, because of reasons about which I can only guess.

# The Storm

It HAD STARTED to snow again in Castle Rock, Colorado, and the footing had become precarious as the earlier melt began to freeze. After completing a successful business appointment, Eric walked to his car in anticipation of a speedy return to his home in Denver. He was not concerned about the storm because he had traveled extensively for many years throughout the Rocky Mountain states. He had experienced a wide variety of weather, including whiteouts from heavy snow in Wyoming, perfect targets for the piercing winds blowing across the flatlands.

As he drove down the street to get to the highway, Eric was impatient with other drivers who, in his estimate, seem to be a bit overly cautious. When entering the freeway, the wheels of his car slipped, reminding him of the hazards of winter driving. Luckily, traffic was light, perhaps a result of the storm's increasing intensity. After driving a mile or two, the lights from Castle Rock were soon a blurred reflection in his rear-view mirror, memories of what had been, faded into the distance.

The snow eclipsed the hillsides and left ghostly white images of trees bent and twisted from the relentless wind blowing across the highway. The terrain was hilly, so the road's undulation was uphill and down, but mostly steadily upward. The new flakes offered better traction, so Eric carefully stepped on the gas peddle to increase the speed of his vehicle.

He could feel the warmth from the car heater and, as he listened to the rhythmic beat of the windshield wipers, his sense of security increased. Upon approaching the crest of the hill, Eric felt a physical and mental transcendence as the beauty of the winter scene surrounded and absorbed him. He did not consider himself a spiritual person. So now, distracting his mind from a subject about which he chose not to think, Eric redirected his mental metaphysics to the warm satisfaction experienced in the success of the meeting from which he has just come.

Suddenly, as his automobile passed over the top of the hill, he could see farther down the highway where several cars had spun out, and positioned all over, blocking the road. Quickly, but carefully, he placed his foot against the brake peddle and pressed down softly, he intended to slow the vehicle to prevent sliding. But his car immediately accelerated as if in rebellion.

His car was not slowing down, and it was gaining speed on the icy surface in response to the pressure applied to the brake. Eric's vehicle's speed increased as it slid forward, headed directly toward two automobiles which faced sideways, and blocked the road two hundred feet ahead of him.

Eric had very little control of his sliding car and could only steer the wheels slightly, offering a limited amount of correction to alter the direction. But the speed of this mass of metal was unaffected racing down and directly toward the other cars below. To move the steering wheel in any radical manner, would send his vehicle spinning into chaos.

He felt helpless, but with only seconds left before the crash, he quickly decided to somehow maneuver the impact of his vehicle simultaneously into the front side of one of the cars and the back side-panel of the other automobile that blocked his projected path. He calculated the total impact would be less for each of the vehicles than that of the full effect of his auto, hitting only one of the other cars.

Strangely, he began to feel relieved as he reasoned the obvious: when things get out of control, what will happen will happen. Sometimes we have no control. A domino effect occurs linking choices from the past to the present.

He could do no more than what he is already doing. From out of his mental state, he became resigned and relaxed his white-knuckle grip on the steering wheel. He became resolved to accept whatever was to be his fate.

As he approached his destiny and was only seconds away, his mind seemed to enter a misty kind of mental fog even though he knew he was at the point of immediate impact. He would wonder later, "Where did my mind go? My eyes were wide open to what was in front of me, yet I did not see either of the other cars move. It was like in one second, two vehicles sat in front of my onrushing car, and the next second, a path opened just wide enough for me to pass through, I never saw those cars move apart."

He could hardly believe what had happened during those few seconds. There was no crash, and the next thing he knew, he raised his foot from the brake peddle, and his vehicle was moving down the highway beyond the cars. The other drivers had separated in time to prevent the crash. At first, he thought he must be delusional or in a dream, but then it seemed as though he had experienced an outstanding miracle of metaphysical magic.

As he later explained to his wife, "I believe I may have been more in shock immediately after this incident than if the impact had occurred. I reassured myself by looking in the rear-view mirror at the cars still spread out on the road, but sure enough, each of them was intact. Between two of the vehicles, a gap had appeared, sufficiently wide enough for my auto to squeeze through."

There was no need to wonder what the occupants of the other cars must have felt and what they would be experiencing once the impact had not occurred. The icy road had prevented him from stopping, so he could only wish them luck on their trip. He then spoke as if talking directly to them, "Thank you for taking such quick action."

It was turning dusk as Eric reached the top of a ridge overlooking the flickering lights of Denver far below. It was still snowing just as densely as when the trip started, but now everything seemed far more beautiful and real. He took a deep breath while feeling exalted with a new sense of life.

# The Circus

DURING BRIEF MOMENTS of separation among shifting cloud sculptures, the sun appears then disappears as if offering a warning. Things are not right in the heavens, but very few people pay close attention. There are always more important things to do—the rituals of commerce mock human life and all the fabulous creations of nature. Benefits disguised as gifts from science pretend to offset the harm done to the earth's ecological system, free-falling toward disaster.

A busy gas station is granted a momentary reprieve from the morning surge of traffic on earth. Drivers inevitably procrastinate until the last moment, denying the energy needs of their vehicles. After the gas tanks are full, the motor vehicles disappear like wisps of vapor into the flowing lanes of traffic. Each relay-pause barely interrupts the unity and constancy of the movement.

Day after day, the machines move one way, then return from the opposite direction. As if mesmerized by the repetitive cadence, the people transform into indispensable parts of the system. They are locked together through the denial of individual choice and conditioned by the dictates of social conformity and the robotic demands of commerce.

A yellow kitten sleeps near a dead house plant in the dirty windowsill overlooking the gas station's front driveway. Outside, energy waste from vehicles dissipates into black smog, cleansing itself through resident city dwellers' tears.

Like a child playing hide-and-seek, the sun pops out of hiding, and the small cat awakens to the undefinable sound of environmental change. The kitten is visually annoyed by that invisible force and peers alertly out the window, angry as if having been mugged for catnip by some sneaky, passerby, rogue-cat.

A large fly, seemingly trapped by the glass window's transparency, voices disapproval of life's injustice and limitations as a fly. The front door is wide open immediately next to the window, but the fly tenaciously refuses to make such a daring escape to freedom through the open passageway.

In response to the sound of the fly, the small ball of yellow fur transforms into an imitation of his hunter ancestry. The cat poses menacingly in readiness for a controlled attack, sure to bring instant death to the fly. The fly is more involved in pretension than the desire to be free—demonstrated by repeatedly attacking the window while buzzing loudly.

A young woman, Maria Adams, dressed nicely in an autumn colored suit, stands in the gas station's office as she quietly awaits the mechanic's report, which looms ominously in her mind.

The smell of petroleum products combines with the scent of the newly painted green concrete floor. The odor is a reminder of Maria's intention to paint the bathroom in the condo where she lives, maybe the same light beige that she has hated since the first day she moved in five years ago, but other people often tell her they like the beige color. Maria feels unexplainably obligated to comply with their decorating taste instead of her own.

Reaching out, she lightly touches the kitten's tense body to reassure herself that with patience, everything will be all right. Her hand passes over the soft fur and the feline's small back arches in response. The savage attack on the stubborn fly becomes forgotten; the kitten begins to purr, and Maria no longer feels so apprehensive.

She is pleasantly surprised when the mechanic returns to say the mechanical problem is not significant; he collects only for gasoline. At the ringing sound of the cash register, the cat moves nervously away, quickly forgetting Maria's gentle caress. When its safety feels threatened, it has no reason to follow an unstated request by a human in need of security.

The cat has become spoiled by the constant attention of motorists who visit the station. It peers out of the dirty rain-marked window in a vigil for the next driver, or, perhaps, preparing for a noisy, unsuspecting fly.

Conrad backs Maria's car out of the garage and leaves the vehicle's door open for her. She feels lucky having not been presented with a mechanic's bill, "Thanks, Conrad."

He advises, "Maybe you should think about getting the motor tuned-up soon."

Nodding in the affirmative, she responds, "I will, Conrad, real soon." She slides across the vinyl seat to position herself behind the steering wheel. He closes the car door. As she slowly starts to pull away, Maria takes a fleeting glance toward the station's front window, but the kitten has disappeared. Maria can only see Conrad shaking his head in sad resignation to his botanical failure as he removes the dead plant for disposal.

In response to Conrad's movements, the fly disappears out the open door but reappears seconds later as if having forgotten something more important than freedom. It vigorously resumes its attack on the window.

As Maria's car joins with the metallic flow of traffic, the seemingly endless combination of colored steel appears to be drawn together like a living body moving in unison to a symphonic rhapsody of blues.

The on-button of the radio responds to Maria's touch, and she listens to a woman sadly singing about betrayal and unhappiness brought to her by love gone wrong. Surprisingly, that unhappy sound of music helps hide the anxiety Maria is experiencing as she contemplates her plans for the evening with her boyfriend, Zack. They are going to the circus, and deep within her bosom, she can feel an unbridled excitement building in anticipation of that event.

She has not been to the circus for over fifteen years, even though it comes to town every October. The immodest promotional billing announces, "The Greatest Show on Earth," but each year, it has come and gone before she seriously takes the time to think about it.

When she was a child, her father would sometimes (rarely) take Maria's sister and her to the circus. The excitement was almost too much to bare for the two small girls once told they would get to go. They worried something might happen once again to prevent them from going. Broken promises brought joy to the point of dread when presented with anything of paramount importance to them, like a proposed visit to the circus. Sometimes the two girls wouldn't even talk to each other about their excitement for fear of their emotions getting too high; the height made them dizzy, and the fall would be devastating. Their emotional risk of disappointment became more urgent than the potential satisfaction found in the experience of a new adventure.

Maria had always admired the trapeze performers at the circus. They seem so independent and free, yet, like earth's ecology, there exists total interdependence of every part of the composition. The performers do incredible feats swinging high above the ground, virtually flying in the air, but a strong man referred to as "catcher" (with taped wrists) is always there to catch them.

In the ecstasy of her daydream, Maria almost misses the turn-off on the street of her workplace. She points the car down the block to the lot where she always parks for the day, but it takes her a minute to consciously recognize her arrival. Like being awakened from a dream, it is challenging to believe a person can drive this far and end up at their destination with only a vague memory of the trip. She wonders to herself if, in this same manner, time might become lost in other repetitious episodes of life.

While driving into the parking lot, she thinks about the large crowd in attendance at the circus that night. After parking, she moves in the direction of the office when a thought spawned in the past flashed through her mind, but it fades away before she can understand it. She whispers to herself, "I hope nothing happens to prevent our going."

While riding up in the crowded elevator to her office, she feels a little faint, but then a friend she has not noticed standing next to her says, "Good morning, Maria." They began talking together about work, and Maria's feelings of faintness disappear. But, business is slow, and the day seems to drag on more deliberately than usual.

Zack is concerned about Maria when he calls her after lunch. He says he is "just checking in," but he wants to make sure Maria is still excited about going with him to the circus. After the conversation's conclusion, she chuckles to herself and feels happy that he took the time to call. When the workday finally ends, she hurries home to eat and get ready for her evening with Zack.

Later, she is startled when the doorbell rings, but of course, it is Zack. Maria grabs her coat and is pulling it on as she opens the door and walks out before he can enter. They are both unusually quiet while driving to the Coliseum for their night at the circus. They both feel an air of shared urgency and excitement emanating from within the vehicle, but they don't mention it during the drive. Instead, they briefly talk about work. Finally, after arriving at their destination, Zack directs the car off the freeway onto the exit ramp.

The cars ahead wait in quiet innocence before circling down the ramp from the highway to the street below. Perhaps it is only in anticipation of the circus that causes Zack to wonder if the cars seem like circus animals. With headlight eyes, each metallic beast of prey stalks the unsuspecting mechanical creature in front of them.

Maria also becomes impatient as she childishly worries, "Will all the seats be gone? Will the circus start while we sit here, helplessly?" She can see people hurrying across the street toward a large building down below. Slowly, the cars begin to move again, and soon Zack parks the vehicle in a lot near the Coliseum.

They dodge oncoming cars as they rush across the street and line up behind happy people waiting in front of the reserve ticket office. After a short wait, they have their tickets and hurry through the portals toward their seats far below the entrance. When arriving at the proper row and seat numbers, Maria excitedly declares, "These are outstanding seats; Zack, good job!" Zack smiles as he answers, unpretenticusly, "They are good seats, aren't they?"

Despite their hurry, the circus hasn't begun yet, so now they must wait. Maria and Zack distract themselves by watching a clown dressed brightly in polka dots. He hurries around waving to the children, especially those who seem too shy or too scared to wave back.

Vendors walk up and down the isles among the seats while making loud howling sounds announcing the sale of souvenirs and things to eat and drink. "Get your BEErr, PEEenuts, and PROgrams, right here!"

Ropes hang down from the ceiling like thick strands of incomplete spider webs waiting for interfacing. In anticipation of the trapeze act, poles stick straight up in the air and are held alert by supporting lines pulling them tightly from the floor.

The pungent smell from the animals' combined expressions of uninhibited spontaneity still lingers from the last performance. Three sizable dirty white circus rings exist side by side on the dirt floor in front of Maria and Zack who's seats are only ten rows above the center ring.

Seats fill up quickly, and three more colorful clowns with bulbous noses and long floppy shoes walk around being silly. Maria can see two rows below her where a small girl, dressed in pink, is standing next to her father. The little child is mesmerized as a clown climbs into the seats in front of her dad and her. The little girl has a slightly sheepish smile and holds tightly to her father's hand. The energetic clown begins talking to several other happy children who are quickly gathering around him.

The little girl's intense stare projects her in amongst the other kids, and she appears to have forgotten the pink cotton candy she holds in her small hand. She has even become oblivious to her father reading a program he holds in his free hand. Suddenly she laughs when the other kids laugh, and Maria laughs too. She feels like she is standing next to her father, who smiles in amusement at his daughter's delight. He has faults, but no matter, she loves him dearly.

At first, lost entirely in thought, Maria doesn't hear the announcer's voice on the public-address system welcoming everybody to "The Greatest Show on Earth." The clowns, who have scattered among the seats, quickly hurry as they climb down to join their colleagues who are loading themselves into a Volkswagen Bug painted brightly to look like a small animal. A clown drives the car to the center arena; then, the announcer counts as one clown after another climbs out of the vehicle. The audience echoes the numbers in unison with him. Finally, it appears all the clowns have vacated the car, but one more suddenly appears in triumph to the applause and glee of the spectators.

The circus has now begun. And as the child in the pink dress had mentally projected herself in among the other kids, Maria and Zack now imagine themselves performing in unison with the circus performers. Even though they never leave their seats, they ride on the backs of lumbering elephants. They fearlessly help in directing wild tigers and lions who roar in protest at the loud cracks of a whip by the trainer who barks out commands to the animals to perform. And when the courageous trapeze artists fly, the couple soars with them.

In all three rings, performers are conducting different acts simultaneously, as if competing for attention. It is hard for Maria to stay alert to all that is happening. At times Maria and Zack hold hands, momentarily grounding themselves back into reality when sharing a glance or a smile before returning to participate in the colorful circus-land as if it needs to be aided by their imagination.

The drums began to roll again, and a chubby ringmaster in a high black hat announces the trapeze acts, three different acts performed all at the same time high above the crowd. Scantily dressed trapeze performers wave their arms in a gesture of tribute as they salute the spectators. Then they quickly scurry up the rope ladders to perch high above the safety nets far below. One man, the catcher, sits on a trapeze away from the other performers. He acts casually, rubbing chalk on his hands as the other performers warm up by swinging back and forth, returning in the air, then dropping onto the platform next to their colleagues. When one of the women takes her turn in swinging out, the men support her return by gallantly placing their hands on the small of her back, then pulling her upright onto the platform.

One time, when the performers are "flying" high above the heads of the audience, Maria says to Zack, "Can you imagine, when I was just a little girl, I had thoughts about running away to the circus and becoming a trapeze artist. But, in truth, you couldn't get me up there like that now for anything." Zack feels a surge of love for Maria in kind of a nostalgic way. He holds her hand throughout the remainder of the act. Memories of experiences and deeds pass through his mind that he, too, has yet to complete and never will if he doesn't take action soon. His work has demanded most of his waking time. He knows that it is his fault and his choice that this is so.

When the last act is over, they make their way back to Zack's car. While they were still inside the Coliseum, it rained outside; now, it feels as if the city became much cleaner during their absence. The smell of the air is fresh and new. They smile in affection as they glance over at each other and talk excitedly about the circus, almost like renewing their lost childhoods.

Zack knows how to escape from the traffic, which is quickly backing up into the main drag. They drive through some back streets, and both become lost in silent thought. Somehow they feel as tired as if it was they who had been performing high above the nets that night. Finally, they speak sparingly to each other, just lingering with the content of their thoughts, each reliving their imagined fright-defying-performance high above the crowd.

Upon arrival at Maria's apartment building, Zack leans over and kisses her goodnight. She whispers, "That was the best circus ever. I had a great evening! Thank you so much."

"It was awesome for me too! It was particularly special sharing it with you; (then he unexpectedly added) I'm glad we got to fly together." She instantly knew what he meant as she remembered feeling a light pressure in the small of her back when he was up there, guiding her to safety back to the ramp high above the crowd.

Suddenly, from out of the blue, while turning to Zack, she announces, "This weekend I am going to paint my bathroom light blue!"

Upon entering her condo, she sat thinking for a long time. Something changed for her that night; an understanding of her life process slowly opened up to her. She no longer felt like a frantic fly pretending to escape from the confinement of a glass window pane. No more would she allow herself to exist like a robot as if not having a personal identity.

Now Maria felt the measured calm of a trapeze artist before leaping off a platform and flying fearlessly into space. She wondered, had she awaken from a long restless sleep and experienced a metamorphosis after living life like a thoughtless fly?

Maria realized that there had never been a need to forgive her father. She excused herself for holding on to the disappointment she felt and carried over through the years after her childhood. Maria knew that freedom and transformation to her true self would come through realizing and accepting personal choice. Life is a responsibility, and she now realizes that it has always been hers to choose.

Maria feels fearless and full of life as she walks through the open door into her business office that next day. She goes directly into her boss's private office to find out about a pay raise promised to her but unfilled. Other people in the office noticed a difference in her demeanor, "committed and fearless," they later said.

A short time after leaving the boss's office, she connects with Zack on the phone, "I'll get right to the point, are we ever going to get married, or what?" Zack is pleasantly surprised. A year later, he brags to a friend that it was one of the best decisions he ever made.

# Discoveries in Nature

LAST SUMMER, Paul went on a fishing trip in the mountains of Colorado. It had not been a difficult choice because he had always enjoyed the remoteness and quiet away from the noise and rush of city life. Paul began the journey while it was still dark outside. He drove directly to his destination a few miles beyond the town of Glenwood Springs. Following the road up the mountain, Paul found a place to park his vehicle close to the creek. He had fished in this beautiful area several times, and it seemed as if the sparkling water came rushing down to greet his return.

Arriving in the early morning has its advantages. The sun was rising in front of him as he fished upstream, casting his shadow behind, helping to prevent the fish from becoming alert to his presence. The cool morning temperature combined with the stream's cold water encouraged him to stay on the rocky embankment to keep his feet dry.

The trout were biting, and the flies and mosquitoes were inactive, leaving Paul without external distractions. He took very little time to become emotionally and mentally involved in this activity, which seemed to whisk him to another life and state of mind.

After fishing for an hour or so, he was instinctively alert to feelings of immediate danger. A shiver ran down his spine as the hair on the back of his neck also responded. Forgotten gifts from his ancient ancestors awakened from deep within in his mind visions of early primitive hunts. It was essential for every hunter to keep their minds and bodies alert to the many dangers found in a hostile environment. To do otherwise would have meant a highly increased probability of being killed and eaten by wild animals.

Paul carefully looked around the surrounding terrain but could distinguish nothing which might contribute to this feeling of immediate danger. A manifestation slowly develops deep from within his inner vision: the magic place where things are never hidden but often unseen. A small deer appeared, initially existing only as an illusion, then slowly emerging into reality as Paul's intuition awakened to harmonize with the existence of the surrounding rocks and dirt terrain. The doe, seemingly born from the mountainside's earth, now stood standing silently about two hundred yards to the right of him.

Paul felt relieved and pleased with the discovery of his new companion but continued to remain apprehensive. He tried to hide his fear by chuckling softly at himself for what he now considered irrational and unnecessary feelings of danger. When dropping his fishing line down into the water again, Paul could not stop feeling a sense of paranoia and anxiety. Thoughts of the deer as mental reinforcement returned to him, a comrade with whom to face the unknown, but when he turned and looked around, he could no longer see the little animal.

Paul could not recall having previous experiences creating such a wilderness reaction, so he forced himself to continue fishing a few minutes more. Then somewhat reluctantly, he decided to return to his automobile, take a break, and eat an early lunch, during which time he could contemplate without distraction this strange experience. After collecting his fishing gear and climbing up the creek bank, he reached a trail that follows the stream down the mountain a mile or so back to his camp.

He had only walked ten or fifteen yards when he spotted mountain lion tracks recently pressed in the dirt by a rather large animal walking on the dusty trail. Paul intensely surveyed the immediate area while considering the probability of this being the time of day that mountain lions might eat lunch. He had no desire to dine at the table of a beast such as this.

After looking around and swallowing his fear, Paul again continued down the trail about ten or twenty yards before becoming aware that he no longer could feel the apprehension experienced earlier and shared with the small deer.

He knew he might be inflating his importance in the world of nature by thinking that a mountain lion had stood on the trail above the creek while observing or following him. That lion may have been stalking the deer. However, this is not the point of the story. Paul asked himself, what is the mechanism that alerts humans to danger, such as those he experienced earlier?

Both the lion and the deer are virtual duplicates from each of their same species, which existed hundreds of years ago. Evolution has done little to change them. They are much the same lion or deer seen by Indians, mountain men, and settlers in the West, who may have walked this same path that Paul followed. His ancestors might have felt threatened, and they certainly would have considered the possibility of their lives ending. If they had not followed their instinctual warnings to stay alert, they might have been killed and eaten by a lion or a bear.

Thousands of years before this, our primitive ancestors must have had the same concerns about their lives when confronted by Sabertooth Tigers or other beasts. However, they would have been more in touch with their natural defensive capabilities called instincts. Paul wondered: Do we all have these instinctual powers lying dormant within our being? He believed the resounding answer to be yes. How could this question be answered otherwise after recently experiencing new capabilities, which may have saved his life earlier that day?

Paul's experience brought with it a responsibility which he pondered during the following days. Does our adoration of science contain the seeds of humankind's undoing? Are we being moved too far away from realizing our true nature found only through self-discovery?

We must rise above our bloated egos created from the perceived importance of existing as a "modern human." Paul had become aware that his experience carried a more significant meaning than the possibility of becoming a tasty snack for a hungry lion.

# Reflections

We often reach out to one another in an effort of mutual sharing. We talk, smile, and sometimes we even touch as if reassuring the miracle of our reflection as seen in other human beings. I remember one fall afternoon when living in this same acknowledged witness. My memory recalls that experience as deep feelings of oppressive emptiness quickly invades my awareness. The mirroring person about whom I speak stands in my mind even now as if in denial of the great joy of reflective miracles, which we each experience from time to time.

One warm afternoon I slowly walked in downtown Denver practicing the art of people watching. I could smell the teasing aroma of the food prepared by local restaurants in response to the lunch-time crowd. It was a lovely day made resplendent by the contrasting assortment of eccentric people who affirmed their reality through collective differences declared by their character and their group, which returned that image to the individual in continuation.

Perfect, I thought in response to an exceptionally proper and polished business lady who rapidly maneuvered among, yet somehow detached from the slower moving crowd. She never touched anyone as she walked with the rhythm and grace of a prima ballerina in performance on some grand stage of life. Yet, in her mind, she had already reached her destination in an office high above the street. Her mouth had a slight smile as if knowing she would soon be looking down on the crowd far below. Upon reaching her lofty vantage, the people and cars seen from above would appear small and without risk.

I then noticed several men wearing dark slacks and white shirts with colorful ties. They hurried down the street with their sports coats draped over their arms as if defiantly out of uniform. At lunch, they would share a pretended independence from their jobs, and through a collective snobbery in response to the appearance of detachment and indifference by their boss. "Why can't he just act like a human being?" They safely critiqued him, knowing he was not there physically among them, "Why can't he come off his high horse?" I stood by in silent response to this organized revolution by people who seemed to imagine themselves to be in other times and other places. And I realized I was part of the pretended anarchy, which exuded the sole purpose of increasing the intensity of the eternal moments which we were each sharing.

As I stood watching, I was distracted by a touch on my shoulder and the sound of a sad voice saying, "Can you spare a quarter, mister?" Words of denial jumped from my mouth in defense as if a tremendous monetary limitation existed. "No, I really..." My words trailed off and seemed to desert me as if placed in the pink leather purse of the "perfect" lady who had recently passed through the awareness of my mind. But now she was nowhere to be found, having ascended into the sky above. The memory and sweet smell of her perfume seemed like an anesthetic confusing my feelings and my thinking.

Standing beside me was a tattered and dingy gray coat harboring a man I viewed as a red-eyed derelict. I started to decline again, "Not today...," but my hand was now groping the change in my pocket, and my fingers clutched the cold metal of a quarter. I mumbled, "Here, take this!" and I dropped the money in his outstretched hand. I tried to avoid touching the unwashed physical member as if it were the hand of death, offering me the plague in thanks for the quarter he had received.

"Thank you." He softly uttered these words as his dark eyes looked directly into my soul. He then slowly turned and limped away with both of his hands in his pants pockets. His shoulders were hunched in the beginning posture of a fetus, waiting for the moment of a new birth. Ironically, his direction was much the same as the proper lady had taken, except the crowded mall seemed to open a path in rejection of him. He willingly accepted his role as a human sacrifice personified through mandatory separation, and he, like she, disappeared into the busy crowd.

My gift to another is often a gift to myself as I experience the joy that accompanies giving, but not this time. I felt despair and oppressive emptiness in my carefully manipulated separation from the stranger. I wanted to put him out of my mind as if he had never existed. I quickly turned to the opulent distractions found inside a nearby jewelry store window. But I could only see the transparent reflection of my image looking back in irreverent mockery.

The thought of "people-watching" returned to my mind. I tried to divert my attention from my reflection in the window to view the vast mass of people I knew were passing behind me. Then, unity replaced separation as the transparent images in the mirror of glass were no longer diffused. I was shocked to see only one person looking back in taunting parody. A dark-gray over-coat covered the man. He had become soiled from sleeping under city viaducts and abandoned buildings' cold doorways; the solitary face looking back was mine.

# A Book

When I boarded the bus, I quickly surveyed the seating and was pleased because I preferred the window seat from which I could watch with detachment the happenings on the street. It was not as if nothing was happening inside the bus: people coming and going, some reading, some deep in thought, many just watched what was going on in the world outside the bus. We were safe, and for the most part, detached, merely silent observers with no immediate threat from the outside world.

It was just such a moment as this that I let my guard down. I had just spotted some boys my age playing football on the grass parking area, and my mind had quickly manifested a moment of fantasy-participation. A pass had been thrown a bit too high, but in anticipation of a grand catch, within my mind, I leaped and stretched my body to its full stature. Anticipation raced through my fingers, and I could feel the exterior of the ball as I reached out—My daydream evaporated when someone sat down on the seat next to me. I could feel them staring at the side of my head. I pretended not to notice, but when the bus stopped, I studied the movements of a lady entering the bus. She had two big sacks of groceries. She sat in a seat farther up the aisle in front of my location and placed her groceries on the seat beside her. I wished that I had brought something to fill the seat next to me.

Close to my leg, I could see what seemed like a giant hand clutching a black imitation-leather book. There was no mistaking it, it was a Bible. The cover showed wear and the pages were bent and soiled. When that man cleared his throat, I knew I was in for it. The demons of mankind always clear their throats in preparation for the verbiage which soon erupts.

He asked rather loudly, "It's nice outside, isn't it?" I pretended he was talking to someone else as I leaned forward to watch a fellow on a racing bike outside the window, but he wasn't racing. His attire was composed of all the proper racing gear, but he had no apparent commitment, seeming content to take his time riding. Now the man next to me leaned his shoulder into mine and remarked on something about the cost of a racing bike. I glanced quickly at him and muttered, "Yea, I guess they do cost a lot."

That was all that he needed: the man was off to the races; he didn't need a bicycle of any kind because he had a Bible which was his vehicle of conveyance. He spoke of the ravages of fire-and-brimstone, and he concluded that I was going to burn in hell if I didn't change my ways.

I pulled the overhead cord which signals the bus driver (and the Bible man next to me) to let me off the bus; I pushed against the man, that conveyor of bad news, because I urgently needed to get into the outer world where I would peacefully walk the remaining two miles to my destination. As the bus driver stepped on the brakes, I thought I was going to end up sitting on the Bible. I quickly recovered, but now I clung desperately to the chrome support bar. As the bus stopped, my weight was thrown forward toward the door. When the door opened, I simultaneously leaped to freedom without touching the steps. I was free again, but in a moment of panic, I quickly looked over my shoulder to be sure the man with the Bible hadn't followed me into the street. I could see him inside the bus, he had a fire in his eyes which were staring menacingly through the window at me, and he was shaking his finger in a gesture of correction and condemnation.

This was many years ago, but to this day whenever I see a sign quoting scripture being held up at a football game, I wonder if it is that same man or one of his Bible-toting colleagues. Why would anybody want to spread such hate like that and blame it on a god as if such a being needed vengeance?

A few days ago I went to a metaphysical bookstore where they were selling crystals. The sales lady who works there said she just couldn't resist some of the beautiful milky looking stones that were for sale. It seemed she had placed on layaway nearly two hundred dollars for what she considered the more choice crystals. As we talked, I question her about why she wanted them. However, for the sake of truth, I intended to expose her belief in mere superstition and hoax. I was better with words then she, so I quickly began to corner her with my logic, the same logic I had used many times before when engaged in a political debate declaring one political party superior to another. Suddenly, I stopped and quickly apologized to her, then abruptly departed from the store. As I moved up the street, my mind shouted at me, "So now we know what became of the Bible man!"

*"So this is hell, I'd never have believed it. You remember all we were told about the torture chamber, the fire-and-brimstone, 'the burning merle.' Old wives tales! There's no need for red-hot pokers. Hell is-OTHER PEOPLE!"*
—Jean-Paul Sartre, *No Exit*

# The Mystery

Each morning I contemplate the mystery often referred to as the sub-conscience. When closing my eyes, my attention is startled by the confusion projected from within my mind. This magic dwelling place of transforming awareness seems to be a contradiction to all previous concepts of reality through which I was schooled during much of the early training of my life.

Surrealistic lines and colors paint landscapes of faraway places never known. Faces, forgotten in the past, now return issuing abrupt greetings as if by planned appointment. Unresolved feelings express sorrow for wrongs committed in life gone by but never actually forgotten.

Having emotionally pledged to always live life truthfully now distracts my attention from the eternal. Meditation is a sacred place to observe the merging of thoughts and feelings into an awareness of mystical unity with all of life.

I can now believe in the rainbow visions which speak of hope across a contrast of stormy skies in the mind's obsessions. The complex reality to which I have become accustomed is denied. Like crayons spreading color on paper depicting a preconceived skyline, my mind strains and then pretends to see the minute detail of an unfathomable eternal reality.

I listen to the soft sounds of friction created by copulating waxen-animals transforming hues of red, yellow, and blue into a new life. As the colors of wax blend against silent backgrounds of black and white, they form new colors demonstrating the evolution of consciousness.

Even now, the waxy sweat of used crayons permeates the air in a fifth-grade classroom where I again sit lost in wonder with all the other little children.

In the continuum of my memory, the sky is like a dark blue window, but a coarse-grained paper reveals a gray sky drawn with thick lines of black outline circling pastel colors. A candle flickers and the luminous intensity is extinguished as my mind denies the reality of living grace.

In the silence of dark memories, I wonder if my childhood sky was really so blue or nearly this resplendent, revealing of so many vibrant colors. Like crayons spreading color on paper depicting a preconceived skyline, my mind strains and pretends to recall the minute details of an unfathomable eternal reality. Then I remember, some of the colors extend erratically outside the black outline, but a voice speaks out, reminding me, "Please, keep the colors inside the lines!"

Now, as I look closely at the streaks of black, the definition becomes apparent in contrast. It is differences which create the picture; it is the black which shows the light. I return to the echoing of my mental discontent and ponder the love and illusions of hate which appear. These impressions are the essential ingredients of humanity; feelings are sparks from eternal fire.

The candle burns brightly now, lending contrast to the night. My eyes want to open and return to the reality from which my travels began, but my heart asks, "What is really the haste? Why must I rush?" The waxen sky of sub-consciousness thunders as if in response to my lack of fear in facing self-accusations of perceived wrongs.

# Dreams

ONE NIGHT WHILE SLEEPING I dreamed of fame and fortune as a deserved benefit, a reward for an incredible idea which had given birth in my dream. But on awakening, I could no longer remember the idea, yet the same exaltation remained as the residue of energy carried over from my dream. And as it continued to magnify in intensity, I resisted mightily, but the adrenaline rush would not go away.

No longer able to restrain myself, I cried out, "I am certainly a genius!" Then, running and leaping down the street repeating, "I'm a genius!" I knew it must have looked like the carrying on of a madman to the lady walking toward me from the opposite direction, but I just didn't care, and yelped again, "I'm a genius!" She was elderly and walked slowly with a cane; she seemed to smile to herself as she listened to my mighty declaration of grand ability. Though somewhat amused she was unimpressed and patiently spoke to me as if I was only a child denying responsibility for the loss of my hat. She spoke firmly, "Let me see your genius!"

I was caught in midair by the impact of the lady's words, and I dropped to earth having been weighed down with a fundamental truth of life. We have no claim to genius defined only by words, dreams, or thoughts; all are soon forgotten in the light of day. Our being is determined by the action taken from thoughts and ideas through which the living life of genius and authenticity has been extracted.

We are what we do! Neither our intentions or pretensions have life without action. Picasso may have had an excellent idea for a painting which could have surpassed in greatness and genius all his other paintings combined. If he had painted the contents of such a vision, the results would surely have been fantastic, yet every artist's divine inspiration remains only an idea or dream until placed on canvas and given true life.

"Take action now before it is too late," the old lady cried out, "Too many unfulfilled dreams lie dead in graves awaiting the imminent arrival of impotent masters. We are the conduit through which dreams and ideas awake, we are the conveyors of the grand energy which is the living source of all life."

I paused for only a moment, I know, yet when I turned, she was nowhere to be seen. Had she just evaporated in a fit of disgust? Had she ever really been here?

In a futile attempt of escape through denial, I turned over in my bed and continued to sleep restlessly.

# Acknowledgements

Martha Baker for editing, encouragement, and friendship; Dr. Patricia Ross who edited while teaching me editing skills, Jan McDaniel for a final edit.

My friends at Socrates meetings, who each in their own way have shared their belief in humanity: Ron Klate, Richard Johnson, Bob Gabrielson, Seth Harris, Gari Westkott, Martha Baker, Jim Ricketts, and Sarah Sparks.

For computer assistance, Susan Sultis.

Encouragement during the five years needed to write the book, John Adams, Mike and Judith Meserve.

Bookcrafters, Joe and Jan McDaniel for guidance and encouragement throughout the publishing process.

Ingram Spark for printing, promoting and distribution of the book.

# Also by the Author

**Authentic Being**
*Dynamic Creativity*

# About the Author

A SIGNIFICANT INFLUENCE in Dr. McCartney's decision to be a writer was a high school English teacher who told him that a homework assignment he turned in would not be given a grade. When asked why, she said the work was too good, and he could not have possibly written it.

The English teacher's rejection was unjust, but he could do nothing about it. However, it didn't take long to realize the value of the gift she had unknowingly given. The backside of her hurtful insult was high flattery when he realized she had, in effect, declared the work superior.

Following six years study, he graduated from the school of theology at Ernest Holmes College. The next two years were given as a Chaplin at two Denver hospitals. Then, back to school at Regis University, where he completed a Master's degree in Adult Education. His path continued in academia with completion of a Doctorate from Emerson Theological Institute.